Iron Eyes the Fearless

Following their robbery of the San Angelo bank, Iron Eyes has just outgunned the Lucas gang when he discovers that the sheriff has been wounded and may not pay out the reward money. Downing most of a bottle of whiskey, Iron Eyes spots another outlaw in the saloon. With time to kill he allows Joe Kane to run and then, like a cat after a juicy mouse, sets out after him into forested Indian territory. He comes under attack from a band of Cheyenne warriors, but although wounded, the bounty-hunter keeps on fighting until his guns are empty. The braves close in. . . .

Tethered to a stake as triumphant chants echo all around him, he awaits his fate silently. He is unafraid. He is Iron Eyes the Fearless.

Iron Eyes the Fearless

Rory Black

A Black Horse Western

ROBERT HALE · LONDON

© Rory Black 2012
First published in Great Britain 2012

ISBN 978-0-7090-9836-2

Robert Hale Limited
Clerkenwell House
Clerkenwell Green
London EC1R 0HT

www.halebooks.com

Typeset by
Derek Doyle & Associates, Shaw Heath
Printed and bound in Great Britain by
CPI Antony Rowe, Chippenham and Eastbourne

Dedicated to my brother-in-law Brian Chard

PROLOGUE

A smouldering inferno of a sky above the remote town of San Angelo was bidding farewell to yet another desert day and heralding the imminent coming of night. Ripples of crimson arches covered the big sky as the distant sun slowly fell into the abyss. A thousand or more people moved quietly through the cooling air as one by one the coal-tar street lanterns along Main Street were awakened once again. Most people were heading to their homes but a hardened few had more interesting things in mind. For the coming of darkness meant that the merciless rays of the sun no longer tormented the flesh of those who walked beneath it.

Amber light spilled out in pools around the high poles which were dotted to both sides of the thoroughfare. Lamps suddenly lit up and cascaded their light from every storefront window and door. For every store owner knew that people are like moths and are drawn to the glowing light of temptation.

The smell of fresh sawdust suddenly traced its way down Main Street as the saloons readied themselves for the busiest part of their days.

Yet for all its activity San Angelo was a quiet town set beside a crystal-clear stream of fresh flowing water flowing down from the forested hills to the north, defying the surrounding desert.

The redness of the sky faded and soon only stars remained in the heavens above the array of hundreds of shingled rooftops. The town was peaceful as most of its kind were along the unmarked line that separated Mexico from Texas, but even in the most somnolent of places there were always a few lawless men who defied the rules. A few drifting outlaws who had no place in respectable, god-fearing towns and were only there because there was nowhere else they could go.

The Lucas gang was a motley crew of three outlaws who had once considered themselves to be cast from the same mould as the Younger brothers, or the Daltons. Yet in all of their bank robberies and stage hold-ups they had never been anything except pale imitations of the more celebrated and successful gangs who plied their infamous trade in the West.

Bob Lucas and his brother Si were all that was left of the five Lucas brothers who had set out to become rich the easy way. After more than five years all they had left in their pockets were a few silver dollars between them and the memories of how their siblings had been killed in one failed robbery after another. Gunsmith Tom Keene had joined the brothers only a year before and, being the only good shot in the gang, had managed to survive.

The bank of San Angelo was not as large as some but its safe was reputed to be full to overflowing. That simple piece of information was all the encouragement the three outlaws, down on their luck, had required to set them on a course for the remote border town a week earlier.

It had been dawn when Bob Lucas led his two followers into San Angelo and now it was sundown. During the intervening hours they had kept their heads low and sipped warm beer in one of the town's many saloons. They had learned the hard way that it did not pay to try and rob a bank during the hours of daylight unless you were good at it. For bank robbers like the Lucas gang it was wiser to await the protection of darkness. They had done so.

After downing their beers the three outlaws rose from the small card table in the darkest corner of the Red Rooster saloon and quietly made their way out into the street. Bob cupped a match flame in his hands and sucked it into his hand-rolled cigarette as his brother rested a shoulder against a weathered upright and stared at the bank standing opposite.

Tom Keene stood between the brothers and said nothing as his thumbs flicked the safety loops off his pair of .44s. He knew his job was to kill and he was very good at it.

The streets were quieter now that the sun had left the sky. The people were thinning out fast as most made their way back to their homes. A few riders were arriving in town from surrounding ranches. These cowboys had only one thought on their minds, and that was to get drunk. The three men said nothing as the cowboys tied their reins to the various hitching poles and marched into the Red Rooster. Along the street other saloons were also finding new customers. The sound of tinny pianos began to waft out into the street from various drinking holes.

'Reckon the bank is ready, Bob?' Si Lucas asked. He took the cigarette from his brother's hand and dragged on it.

'Yep,' Bob Lucas answered in a low drawl. 'Reckon so.'

Keene moved to the edge of the boardwalk and spat out into the street. 'Ya want me to take the horses up the street aways, Bob?'

'Yep.' Bob nodded. 'Me and Si will head on up through the alley and break in through the back way of the bank, Tom.'

Keene stepped down and pulled the reins free of the hitching rail. His cold eyes looked at the brothers as he turned the three horses. 'How long do ya figure it'll take to crack the safe?'

Si pulled his vest away from his shirt to reveal a single stick of dynamite jutting up from his breast pocket. It had a short fuse cord poking out of its

10

top. The outlaw smiled.

'Ain't gonna take very long at all, Tom. Ain't gonna take very long at all once this thing goes off.'

Tom Keene gave a nod. 'I'll have the horses waiting up by that closed dress shop yonder. When I hear the bang I'll wait to see who comes looking and kill 'em. Then I'll bring the nags around back of the bank. OK?'

'Fine,' Bob Lucas said. 'Mighty fine.'

Both brothers stepped down on to the sand next to Keene. Bob Lucas turned and looked at the hardened gunman.

'Ya better keep an eye open for the sheriff, Tom.'

'Always do.' Keene led the horses away from the hitching rail and walked across the dark street to a building set a couple of doors up from the small bank. The nearest street lantern was forty feet away, allowing a man to wait unseen in the shadows outside the small store with a window filled with fancy female apparel. Like most of the wooden structures at the far end of the main street, apart from the saloons, it was in darkness.

As Keene reached the dress shop and looped the reins over its long hitching pole he watched the last of the Lucas brothers disappear up into the alley next to the bank.

Nobody seemed to notice the man seated on the boardwalk step facing the three horses. Keene liked it that way. The saloons were drawing men like flies but no one ventured to where the outlaw waited.

11

Like a nervous jack rabbit Keene kept glancing along the street to where he saw the lamplight spilling out from two half-shuttered windows. The sheriff's office was quiet but Keene knew that when the explosion rocked San Angelo more than one lawman might come out to investigate.

That was what always happened. That was why he had shot and killed three men wearing tin stars during the time he had spent with the Lucas brothers. Keene knew that towns without their hired peace-makers were like chickens with their heads cut off. They were helpless.

He kept watching from beneath the brim of his Stetson. If there was going to be trouble he would stop it in its tracks, as he always did. He knew his job but was always troubled that his partners were not too capable of doing theirs.

Keene was about to put a cigar between his teeth when he heard the sound of spurs ringing out. The outlaw stared through the gaps between their three horses, but saw nothing. He looked to both sides but did not see anyone. Yet the haunting sound of the spurs filled his ears.

Then it faded.

After what had felt like an eternity of waiting the muffled sound of the blast rocked the wooden boards beneath his backside. Smoke billowed out from around the bank's front door, but somehow not one pane of glass on the bank's façade had even been cracked.

'Si's getting better at blasting safes,' Keene said as he watched the reaction along the long dark street.

Men came out from every saloon in the street but they did not interest the outlaw. Drunken cowboys posed no threat to men who knew how to handle their weaponry as he did. The lawmen were a different matter, though. When Keene saw the door to the sheriff's office open and spill light across the street he rose and drew one of his .44s. He kept squinting and saw two figures rush out into the cool evening air.

Both men saw the smoke escaping from the bank around its sturdy front door. The sound of Winchesters being cranked into readiness filled Keene's ears.

Knowing that the three large horses were masking him from the eyes of the people in the saloon doorways Keene raised, cocked and aimed his gun at the two men running towards the bank. As they ran beneath the street lanterns their tin stars sparkled like diamonds. Keene fired and saw the first figure drop his rifle, then buckle and fall. Within a mere heartbeat Keene cocked and fired again. The second man staggered, then crashed down into the dust before forcing himself up on to one knee. Keene cocked and fired again. This time the lawman flew backwards.

The outlaw heard gasps of horror sounding up and down the street as cowboys ran back into the saloons.

13

Knowing that there was no time to lose, Keene pulled the reins to the three horses free and led them up into the clouds of smoke and dust that filled the alley next to the bank.

The smoke cleared as Keene reached the back yard of the bank with the horses. At the same moment the Lucas brothers ran clear of the open rear door of the building, carrying two large canvas bags filled with banknotes.

'How'd it go?' Keene asked.

'Like a dream, Tom.' Bob Lucas laughed.

Keene held the horses in check as Si and Bob mounted up before throwing himself up on to his own saddle.

'Any trouble?' Si asked Keene, as he hung the bag from his saddle horn. 'Heard shooting.'

'Had to kill me some starpackers.' Keene grinned.

Bob Lucas pointed a finger to where a gap in the yard fencing led to a back street. 'Let's go thataway. C'mon.'

The three riders spurred and started across the long-grass-covered yard of the bank's property towards a substantial gap in the wooden fencing.

Then, directly ahead of them, a figure suddenly appeared in the gap of the fence. The man lit a cigar, then tossed the match aside as his hands dragged both his Navy Colts from his pants belt and cocked their hammers.

Bob slowed and looked to his brother. 'Who in

14

tarnation is that, Si?'

There was no time to answer. No time to do anything except see the flashes of thunder which came from both barrels of the cigar-smoking man's guns.

More flashes of lethal lead cut through the darkness at the horsemen. Before any of the three bank robbers knew what was happening their horses crashed into the sand. Fountains of blood showered over the spilled outlaws as they ate sand.

'Kill him,' Bob Lucas screamed out, his left hand clawing to where his bag of money had landed.

The evening breeze caught the long, dark mane of hair of the man who was walking towards them.

'Kill me?' the low rasping voice said as smoke trailed from the man's teeth. 'I don't die easy, boy.'

Bob Lucas stretched out his left hand for the bag. Then two more blasts came from the Navy Colts. Lucas screamed out and rocked on his knees as his wide-open eyes stared at what was left of his hand.

Every one of his fingers had been shot clean off. Only bloody stumps and skinless bone remained.

'He's shot my hand off. Kill him,' Bob Lucas yelled out feverishly. 'Kill him good.'

Si had hit the ground head first. He was dazed. He dragged himself up from beside his dead horse, then gasped when he saw the bullet hole in its skull. He swung around and went for his gun.

Then he saw the tall emaciated figure emerge like a ghost from the shadows and pause. The outlaw felt his throat tighten as his eyes focused on the hideous sight.

'Iron Eyes,' he stammered.

'I told ya to kill him,' Bob Lucas repeated his venomous screaming at his stunned men. 'Don't either of ya hear me? Kill him.'

Si Lucas kept staring at the bounty hunter. 'That's Iron Eyes, boys. We're as good as dead.'

'I don't care who ya think that is. Just draw that hogleg and kill the bastard, Si,' the elder Lucas brother demanded.

Tom Keene shook the fog from his head and pulled at his leg, trapped under the side of his stricken mount.

'What ya say, Si?' he groaned as he managed to free himself and get back to his feet holding his head. 'What ya say?'

'Look.' Si Lucas pointed at the bounty hunter who was still standing with his smoking guns in his bony hands aimed straight at the three men. 'Look at him, Tom. Ain't that Iron Eyes?'

Keene steadied himself. He screwed up his eyes and then saw the eerie figure. He felt his heart quicken. Si Lucas was correct.

'It surely is, Si,' Keene said. He made to draw both his guns.

Two more shots rang out from the guns of Iron Eyes. Both hit Keene in the chest, sending him flying backwards. The dead outlaw lay at the feet of Si Lucas, whose hand hovered above his holstered gun's grip.

'Ya ain't gonna kill me is ya, Iron Eyes?' Si Lucas asked as he felt his pants dampen. 'I'm no match for the likes of you.'

'Ain't nobody ever gonna listen to me?' Bob Lucas got to his feet and shook his fingerless hand around. 'Draw ya gun and shoot the varmint, Si.'

'Are ya loco, Bob?' Si swallowed hard.

Bob Lucas turned and snarled at the bounty hunter. 'Ya don't scare me, Iron Eyes. Ya hear me?'

'A dead man could hear, ya, Lucas.' Iron Eyes squeezed both triggers again.

Both outlaws fell in crumpled heaps next to the two bags of money that they had just stolen. The bounty hunter walked to where the dead men and animals lay and only then did he push his guns down in behind his belt buckle.

The sheriff staggered around the corner holding a .45 in one hand as his other pressed against the bleeding hole in his shoulder. The sickening sight which greeted him stopped him in his tracks. Then Iron Eyes turned to look at the lawman and his eyes widened even more.

The sheriff gasped and took a step backward. 'Holy Mary.'

'About time ya got here, Sheriff.' The bounty hunter pulled out a Wanted poster and shook it before pushing it into the blood,, stained shirt of the lawman. 'I think you'll see that these three men are wanted dead or alive and I'm due two hundred dollars in bounty.'

17

'Who are ya?' the sheriff asked.

'I am Iron Eyes,' the bounty hunter answered. 'Saw these critters eyeing up the bank and then recalled I had me paper on them.'

'Why didn't ya just round them up and bring them to me?' the wounded lawman asked.

'Why didn't I do what? Hell. They was wanted dead or alive, Sheriff,' Iron Eyes said, smoke trailing from his mouth. 'I don't take prisoners.'

ONE

San Angelo was stunned. None of its mostly law-abiding people had ever known anything like the whirlwind in human form that had suddenly appeared within their boundaries and dispatched the three bank robbers with such ease. The skeletal figure who looked more dead than alive seemed to have just arisen from the very bowels of Hell itself, like a demonic avenger sent by Satan to rock the foundations of everything these innocent people believed in. There was a strange power in Iron Eyes which frightened all who cast their eyes upon him. He looked nothing like a normal man looked. Heavily scarred from a lifetime of battles, his very appearance chilled the souls of those who looked into his bullet-coloured eyes.

More than an hour had passed since the bounty hunter wiped out the Lucas gang behind the bank. The old clock on the church steeple said it was nearly seven in the evening, yet it felt like a lifetime since the brutal blasts of his Navy Colts had echoed off the wooden buildings.

The tall thin man had roamed from one saloon to another, downing whiskey in all of them as he waited for the town's only doctor to cut the lead out of Sheriff Dan Landon's shoulder. Iron Eyes knew that he was owed $200 in blood money and intended collecting every last penny of it before he left San Angelo in search of fresh, more profitable prey. The bounty hunter had started to realize that the lawman's wound must have been a lot worse than he had first supposed otherwise Landon would have been back on his feet by now.

The streets were still cloaked in shadow and buzzing with the terrified whispers of those who watched the tall man in the long blood-stained trail coat as he moved from one drinking hole to another. The sound of his spurs echoed in the air as Iron Eyes walked back into the lantern light of the last saloon on Main Street. The Red Rooster was a reasonable size compared with all of its competitors.

The noise of its tinny piano had resumed since the mayhem had ceased. Iron Eyes moved along the boardwalk towards it like a floating ghost, with a thin black cigar gripped in his sharp teeth. The scent of stale tobacco smoke drew him towards the saloon like a fly drawn to an outhouse short of lime. He reached its swing doors and paused to look over them, like an eagle pondering its next kill.

He sucked in smoke and allowed it to fill his lungs as he watched the men and females within the confines of the Red Rooster going about their nightly rituals. It did not take long before Iron Eyes himself was noticed. As his hideous features peered into the Red Rooster the piano-player stopped playing and the short fat man scurried away. The sound of drunken talking ended as abruptly as the music. Iron Eyes spat the remnant of his smoke away and pushed a fresh cigar between his teeth. He then rested his bony hands upon the doors, pushed them apart and entered the saloon.

Only the sound of his spurs filled the interior of the long bar room. He heard the sharp intake of breath as men and bargirls all gasped in shared fear. As the doors rocked on their hinges behind the tail of his long trail coat Iron Eyes drew a thumbnail across a match head and cupped its flame.

He inhaled the smoke deeply. His eyes darted around the saloon. If there was even a hint of danger within the Red Rooster's four walls he would know instantly. He would know and would react with lethal expeditiousness. Only a few had ever managed to get the drop on Iron Eyes. He wore the scars of those mistakes for all to see.

As were all of the other drinking holes he had visited since leaving the sheriff in the capable hands of the doctor, the Red Rooster was filled, mostly with cowboys and a few reasonably aged females in fancy dresses. As in all the other saloons in San

21

Angelo, he sensed the mixture of fear and contempt at the mere sight of him.

He was used to that.

He had lived with that all his life.

Iron Eyes had learned long ago that people never like seeing the more monstrous-looking of God's creations. They liked to hide all monsters away from view behind high walls in cages. They preferred to pretend that there were no men or women who were truly horrifying in appearance. Whatever the reason for the difference, whether it be that Nature had dealt them a bad hand or whether it was due to a lifetime of collecting injuries, they simply hated to admit that there are some people not cast in God's image. Some who are, sadly, just different.

Iron Eyes blew the match flame out and tossed the blackened two-inch sliver of wood over his shoulder. He pulled the front of his dust jacket apart to reveal the gun grips set against his flat belly. Both grips jutted out from his pants belt. Unlike most men who roamed the West Iron Eyes never used a gunbelt with holsters.

He wanted to feel his guns against his guts. To know always that they were there, waiting for his bony hands to drag them clear so he could start shooting.

The sound of his spurs rang through the heart of the Red Rooster as he walked slowly across the sawdust-covered boards towards the long bar counter. Two bartenders were standing like statues, fearfully watching his approach. Neither man took his eyes from the bounty hunter until he reached the counter and lifted his left boot to rest upon its brass rail.

'What'll it be?' the nearer of the barmen asked.

'Whiskey.' Iron Eyes placed a coin down, then pointed at a bottle with its paper seal still intact across its cork. 'That 'un.'

The bartender obliged and placed the bottle down next to the coin. 'Would ya like a whiskey glass?'

'Hope.' Iron Eyes grabbed the bottle and smashed its neck against the edge of the bar counter. A gasp went around the patrons of the saloon. 'A beer glass will do just fine.'

The bartender nervously placed a large glass down next to the coin. He said nothing as he carefully slid the coin toward himself and then moved back to the cash drawer.

Iron Eyes filled the glass with whiskey, then pushed the half-empty bottle away from him. 'The bar gals can have the rest of this.'

The females gleefully rushed through the crowd of cowboys to the bottle with the broken neck and started to bang the counter with their small hands. Both bartenders filled small thimble glasses with the amber liquor as they watched the tall bounty hunter move away from the counter, making for the darkest part of the saloon.

Although Iron Eyes did not know it, he was

actually sitting on the same chair that Bob Lucas had polished with his pants only just over an hour before.

The thin man sat with his back to the wall and stared through the shadows at the people who slowly started to talk again once they could not see his face. He sipped at the whiskey and just watched from the dark corner of the Red Rooster. He knew only too well that its patrons could not see his hideous features, so they would soon relax.

After a while more men entered the saloon. Some he recognized from other saloons along the street. Others were unknown to the deadly bounty hunter.

Each face he saw was instantly evaluated in his mind. If he had ever seen its likeness on a Wanted poster he knew he would immediately remember not only the name but the man's value. Dead or alive value, that was.

Since Iron Eyes had first turned from hunting animals for their pelts to hunting men for their bounty he had seen hundreds of Wanted posters. Somehow every one of them was branded into his memory. Each crude image was carved into a mind that was as cold as ice.

The saloon got busier as the wall clock chimed out eight times. It was as though the men and women inside the Red Rooster had forgotten all about the strange deadly creature sitting in the darkest part of the saloon, sipping on his whiskey.

24

Out of sight, out of mind had never been more true.

Seated beneath the staircase, he was masked from view to all but those with the keenest eyesight and curiosity. Iron Eyes liked it that way.

He had managed to consume half the contents of the glass and was searching for another long black cigar in his deep pockets as he pondered how long he would have to wait before he would be paid for his deadly handiwork. Iron Eyes knew only too well that it required the signature of the sheriff on a receipt to allow the bounty to be paid.

Without it he would get nothing.

The bounty hunter forced a fresh cigar into his mouth, then reached to his shirt pocket and plucked a match from its weathered fabric.

Three more men pushed the swing doors apart and entered. They approached the bar counter. Iron Eyes studied them as he had studied every one of the men he had set eyes upon since entering the Red Rooster. Two were caked in dust but had fancy gear on. He knew instantly that they were cowboys looking to sow some wild oats. The third was different. He had the dust of a long ride covering his trail gear. Iron Eyes turned the match so that its blue tip was next to his sharp thumbnail and considered the third man as his mind raced.

Iron Eyes knew the third man seemed familiar.

The lean bounty hunter eased himself up on his chair, placed the glass of whiskey down on the card table and squinted at the dust-covered man. Even though his face was covered in trail dirt Iron Eyes could see he was nervous.

Real nervous.

The bounty hunter knew why.

His thumbnail scratched the match.

A spark became a flame. It rose a couple of inches up into the air before it calmed down. The dust-caked man at the bar counter looked to where the erupting match lit up the shadowy corner of the saloon. Suddenly he looked even more afraid.

He had recognized the cruel face lit up by the flame of the match as Iron Eyes inhaled the smoke into his lungs.

Swallowing hard, the nervous man pulled his hat brim down as far as it would go and toyed with the idea of either running back into the street or remaining in the crowd. It was clear to the sharp-eyed bounty hunter that neither option sat well in the mind of the man.

Iron Eyes blew the match out.

He had not blinked once since seeing the reaction of the man standing in the company of so many cowboys. Iron Eyes knew that the man had spotted him, just as he had recognized whom he was looking at.

'Joe Kane.' Iron Eyes heard himself whisper as his brain calculated the worth of the outlaw. 'Wanted dead or alive. $500 bounty. A tidy sum.'

Joseph Albert Kane felt his heart pounding like a war drum inside his shirt. The match had stayed alight just long enough for him to see the cruel twisted face. The face that he, like so many other outlaws, had heard about.

The face of Iron Eyes.

He shuffled behind two drunken cowboys. Neither cowpuncher had any inkling that he was being used as a shield by the outlaw as he tossed a coin on the bar counter and accepted a glass of suds. He swallowed the beer fast, then rubbed his mouth along his sleeve.

If all the tales Kane had heard about the infamous bounty hunter were true then it was highly unlikely that he was going to be able to leave the saloon alive. The outlaw tried desperately to calm himself down. He turned his back and discreetly checked his six-shooter. Sweat started to run down his face, leaving tanned tracks through the dust which covered his face.

He had to get out.

Get back to his horse at the hitching rail.

Kane looked at the swing doors. They were roughly twenty feet away. Twenty feet of clear air. Kane knew that it might as well be a hundred miles. He would never make it.

Not without being riddled with bullets.

Still watching the outlaw, Iron Eyes took another mouthful of whiskey and swallowed the fiery liquid. He sucked on the cigar again. Smoke drifted from between his teeth as he pulled one of his Navy Colts from his belt and opened its chamber. Fully loaded.

He sat back, rested the weapon on the stained green baize, then ran a finger over his scarred lips. A thought came to him.

Was it worth killing Joe Kane here in San Angelo?

He was still waiting to be paid for the Lucas gang. If the old sheriff took a turn for the worse the bounty might never be paid.

He kept staring at Kane.

Bullets cost fourteen cents each. Was it worth wasting even more of them with no chance of getting rewarded?

An idea occurred to Iron Eyes. Maybe he ought to let Kane ride and then just follow until they got close to another town before he killed him. A town with a sheriff who was able to sign for the reward money.

That was it.

Let the stinking varmint go, catch up with him later, then kill him. Iron Eyes nodded to himself and dropped his cigar into a spittoon at his right boot. A hiss sent a small trail of smoke upward as burning tobacco mingled with a quart of spittle.

The bounty hunter heard the sound of feet running across the boards outside the saloon window. His eyes moved from the outlaw to the swing doors.

'Iron Eyes.'

The bounty hunter heard his name being shouted out over and over again. He rose to his feet as a barefoot young lad of about fifteen years came bundling through the swing doors of the saloon.

'Is ya in here, Iron Eyes?' the boy bellowed.

Suddenly Joe Kane made his move. He pushed two of the cowboys towards the corner where Iron Eyes was seated. Then the outlaw drew his gun, ran to the boy and grabbed him around the neck. He hauled the youngster backwards as his gun kept pointing to where the bounty hunter was sitting.

'Listen up, Iron Eyes. One move and I'll blow this kid's head off,' Kane snarled. 'Stay where ya are until I rides clear of this town. Ya savvy?'

Iron Eyes stood and defiantly stepped out of the shadows.

'I savvy, Joe.'

Joe Kane felt the swing doors against his shoulder. 'Ya know me?'

'I do.' Iron Eyes nodded.

Kane pushed the boy towards the bounty hunter and bolted out into the street. The lad stumbled and slid through the sawdust between the legs of cowboys until he was staring up into the horrific face of the bounty hunter. The boy swallowed hard as the sound of thundering hoofs filled the Red Rooster.

'Are ya Iron Eyes?' the boy stammered.

'Yep.'

'The sheriff done up and took a turn for the worse,' the boy blurted out. 'The doc said ya ain't gonna get paid for all the killing ya done until old Landon wakes up. Might be a couple of days. Doc drugged him up too much.'

The bounty hunter inhaled, walked to the swing doors and stared out into the dark street.

'Damn it all.' Iron Eyes let the breath go.

The boy scrambled away on all fours and disappeared under the swing doors and over the tall figure's boots.

Every eye inside the Red Rooster watched as the thin man brooded over the news. Iron Eyes pushed the swing doors apart and walked into the street.

He stood like a statue for a few moments. Then he tilted his head to look to where his high-shouldered palomino stallion was standing, hitched to rail. The sound of his spurs rang out as Iron Eyes walked to the rail and stepped down to the sand. He tugged his reins free, held on to his saddle horn and lifted his left boot.

Iron Eyes mounted and sighed.

His eyes narrowed and looked at the dust still hanging on the night air. Dust kicked up by Joe Kane's fleeing horse's hoofs.

'C'mon, horse,' he said. 'We got us an outlaw to kill.'

He tapped his spurs.

The stallion walked off into the hanging cloud of dust.

TWO

Fear can drive even the most weary of men ever onward in their frantic desire to escape the retribution they know is coming as surely as day follows night. Outlaw Joe Kane was no hero, like most of his breed. He liked to kill when the odds favoured him and there was little chance of his target even seeing his deadly gun. Kane had ridden for nearly a day and a half in his vain attempt to shake off Iron Eyes. He had only managed to survive this long because his hunter had no desire to kill him until they were within spitting distance of a town.

A town where Iron Eyes could collect his bounty.

If it were possible for a horse to sense the terror of its master then the lathered-up grey beneath Kane's saddle could not have reacted better. The fourteen-hang gelding had thundered on through its own pain across the featureless prairie until it had reached the forested slopes of the hills which led to Indian territory. Kane knew that he was

31

taking his life in his hands by entering this land, yet he feared Indians a lot less than he feared the deadly Iron Eyes.

The forest grew more and more dense as the outlaw desperately whipped his mount's shoulders with his rein leathers. Soon there would be sanctuary where he might allow his horse to rest as he lay in wait for the deadly bounty hunter.

Iron Eyes too found that the trees were growing ever more closely togather as he drove his spurs into the flanks of his palomino stallion and forced it to keep moving through the unfamiliar terrain.

Iron Eyes had not wanted his chosen target to head this way when he had allowed Kane to flee the Red Rooster. This was the wilderness, nowhere near a town. He had not wanted to chase Kane into the middle of nowhere. To kill him here would be pointless. His carcass would rot long before he could get it to another town to collect the reward money. The body had to be recognizable if he were to be paid his blood money.

A thousand thoughts drifted through the bounty hunter's mind as he forged on through the trees. Maybe he could capture Kane and take him alive to the next town? Iron Eyes had never once opted for the alive part of dead or alive. It did not sit well with him. He gritted his teeth and drove his horse on.

Maybe he could capture Kane alive and then kill him outside the next sheriff's office? That was an option. The outlaw would be mighty fresh then.

Fresh and looking like his image on the Wanted poster. Iron Eyes nodded to himself and kept spurring.

The trouble was, he had not caught even a glimpse of his prey since Kane had headed into the forest.

It was not quite noon and the sun was at its highest, but only fleeting rays managed to penetrate the thick canopies of dark-green leaves far above him. Nevertheless Iron Eyes could sense that he was getting closer to Kane with every beat of his cold, merciless heart.

The scent of a terrified outlaw was nothing new to the bounty hunter. He had smelled that scent a hundred times before and realized that soon he would be able to finish off the fleeing man who was wanted dead or alive.

Again he considered the fact that he was nowhere near the next border town; indeed he was getting further and further away with every passing minute.

Why was Kane heading this way?

The question troubled Iron Eyes.

The forest was getting more and more untamed as the valiant palomino stallion obeyed its master and kept on riding into the dense growth. Brambles and razor-sharp vines hung across the trail that Iron Eyes was following, but they had already been parted by the outlaw's horse as its master tried to escape the justice that he knew was getting closer and closer behind his horse's tail.

Iron Eyes had been riding throughout the night and for another half-day and only paused three or four times to allow his mount to drink from one of his many canteens.

The hoof-tracks were clear to a man with honed eyesight. They were heading to somewhere at the top of the tree-covered hill, where a handful of rocks and boulders marked the summit of the small rise. The bounty hunter did not know it, but more similar hills lay beyond the one that he could now make out above him.

Iron Eyes was thirsty. He dragged rein and brought the powerful horse beneath him to an abrupt halt. Dust kept on moving up to where the bounty hunter knew the outlaw would be waiting for him. Waiting with a long rifle to try and pluck his relentless pursuer off his saddle with a clean shot.

Instinct told the bounty hunter that he was already in range of a man with a Winchester, but that did not trouble him. He swung his long right leg over the neck and head of his mount and slid off his saddle. A small cloud of dust rose from around his mule-eared boots.

Iron Eyes moved like a panther around his horse and studied the wounds made by his brutal spurs. Yet there was no hint of remorse in the tall emaciated figure. He lifted the flap of one of his saddle-bag satchels and poked his long thin arm into it.

His fingers found what they had been seeking.

They pulled out a full bottle of whiskey. Iron Eyes studied the bottle, then drew its cork free with his small sharp teeth and spat it into the palm of one hand. The other hand lifted the bottle up until its neck was at his cracked, scarred lips.

For more than a minute the bounty hunter drank. The fiery liquor had no effect on him at all. In all his days he had never managed to get drunk like other men, no matter how much whiskey he consumed.

He lowered the bottle and then sighed heavily.

His eyes darted back up between the trees to the place from where he could smell the man's sweat drifting down. He smiled.

He replaced the cork and dropped the bottle into his saddle-bag. His hands searched the deep bullet-filled pockets of his trail coat until they came upon the crumpled paper. He shook it until it unfolded, then stared at the crude image of the man he was hunting. A man he knew nothing about except for the fact that he was worth $500 dead or alive. Joe Kane was a murderer of women mostly but had managed to add horse-stealing to his long list of crimes over the previous five years. It seemed that the outlaw was wanted in three states and a territory, but no one had ever even tried to bring him to book.

Until now.

If Iron Eyes had been paid for killing the Lucas

gang he might not even have bothered to hunt Kane. He was tired, but he refused to admit it to himself.

It amused the bounty hunter when he recalled the expression on Kane's face when he had recognized him back in the Red Rooster. When Kane had seen the gaunt figure with his long, black, matted mane of hair and had then looked into the scarred face he had almost died of fright there and then.

For a day and a half they had both ridden across country until they had reached the forest. One rider chasing and the other being chased. The hunter and the hunted.

It had not mattered how many shots Kane had fired back at the gruesome creature who followed him, Iron Eyes would never quit until it was over.

'Ya a dead man, Joe,' Iron Eyes whispered. He pushed a cigar into the corner of his mouth and struck a match with his thumbnail. Smoke filtered through his teeth as he stared at the Wanted poster. 'Dead and I bet ya knows it.'

For one more time since they had headed out of San Angelo the bounty hunter decided it was time to rest his mount. He hooked the stirrup of the raised fender on the saddle horn and undid the cinch straps of the ornate Mexican saddle. When the straps fell free Iron Eyes hauled the heavy saddle off the horse's back and dropped it down on the ground.

Steam rose from the back of the sweat-soaked

horse. The bony hand pulled the blanket free, then turned it over and started to wipe the suds off the stallion's back.

'I reckon this is kinda overdue,' Iron Eyes said to the horse, who watched his every movement. 'I forget that ya a good horse coz I'm used to riding them pitiful Injun ponies. Ya lucky, really. I used to ride them into the ground and then let the critters die.'

The horse snorted and its ears pricked forward.

Iron Eyes dropped the blanket and hauled one of his Navy Colts from his belt. He cocked its hammer. He eased himself next to the noble head of the animal.

'What ya heard, boy?' the bounty hunter asked as smoke billowed from his mouth. 'Heard old Joe trying to get closer or maybe ya heard something else.'

Whatever it was that had alerted the horse the tall thin man could not see anything but stout trees and dense brush. The tall man ran a hand down the nose of the horse as his eyes vainly darted around the area in search of whatever it was that had made the sound that had alarmed his mount.

'Can't be Joe,' Iron Eyes whispered. 'He ain't brave or loco enough to come looking to shoot me.'

Then he heard something to his right. A dried twig snapped and birds rose up and took flight. Yet before the bounty hunter could aim another noise came from somewhere behind him.

'That's kinda curious.' Iron Eyes drew his other Navy Colt and levelled them in both directions.

A cruel smile etched the scarred face. Iron Eyes pulled the cigar from his mouth and stared ahead through its smoke.

'Whatever they is there must be two of 'em,' he drawled. Then another sound came from high on the hill top.

It was a scream.

A man's scream.

Then Iron Eyes heard a high-pitched humming noise coming towards him. He had heard that sound many times before. It was arrows.

Arrows in flight.

Iron Eyes pushed the stallion aside as the first of the deadly projectiles rained in on him. Pain carved its way through him as one struck and pierced his flesh. The emaciated man was knocked off his feet.

His body hit the ground hard and lay entwined in vicious brambles. The sound of twigs snapping filled his ears. They were coming to finish him.

Iron Eyes looked at the arrow shaft in his chest.

'I hate Injuns,' he moaned.

THREE

Flashes of light traced along the wooden arrow shafts as they were propelled from all sides. Suddenly the tree he was standing beside was peppered with the lethal projectiles. Defiantly the tall figure gripped his Navy Colts and tried to steady himself as blood spurted out from where the first of the arrows had embedded itself in his lean chest. More arrows came flying through the dense green undergrowth in search of their bewildered target. Leaves were ripped from branches as the flint arrowheads carved their way through the midday air.

Iron Eyes swallowed hard and leaned against the tree before blasting two shots blindly into the wall of lush vegetation. As the wounded bounty hunter rested against the trunk of the stout tree he could feel the arrowhead catching on its bark. The arrow had gone clean through his emaciated body.

More blood spat from around the wooden shaft

and over its feathered flight.

'I bin skewered again, damn it,' Iron Eyes growled before firing his guns again. 'Every damn time I runs into Injuns they shoots me. Damn, I sure hates Injuns. Hates 'em even more than they hates me.'

He could taste blood in his mouth. He spun on his heels and blasted both his guns at targets he could not see. If he was hitting any of them they were keeping real quiet about it. Iron Eyes kicked out at the muscular stallion and forced it to run away from where he stood.

A mere heartbeat later another dozen arrows embedded themselves into the tree beside which his mount had been standing only a few seconds earlier. He crouched, then fired as his keen hearing detected yet more arrows leaving their bowstrings.

It was as though the forest was alive with swarms of crazed hornets, each seeking only one thing. To kill the intruder who had dared invade their land. The arrows came close to achieving their goal as they whizzed just over his head.

'Ya starting to make me angry,' the bounty hunter yelled out before blasting two more shots in the direction from where the last volley of arrows had come. Chunks of the bushes were severed by his lead and flew heavenward.

Turning, Iron Eyes stumbled over his saddle. He pushed himself back up until he could feel the ground under his boots again. He had to keep moving, he told himself as he staggered through the bushes of brambles. He felt the thorns tearing at his jacket and then his skin but he kept moving.

The various types of trees were close together and had never seen an axe blade, he told himself. That was good for a man who needed all the cover he could get to escape being hit by even more arrows from his still unseen attackers. He was panting like an old hound as he rested beside two entwined tree trunks and vainly tried to muster his thoughts into a course of action.

It was useless. No matter how hard he tried to think his brain refused to work. It was like being half-asleep. His mind was filling with a strange fog. A fog he did not recognize.

The tree trunks vibrated as yet more arrows hit them. They were coming from all directions. He was surrounded by archers all intent on turning his body into a pincushion.

Iron Eyes squeezed his triggers again in pitiful reply. He dragged himself to his full height and rested his back against the tree trunk. Again his body arched in agony as the arrowhead caught on the rough tree bark behind him. He had to have a plan, he kept telling himself. A plan not to only escape his nightmare but to survive. He was getting desperate. Time was running out and he knew it.

'Think!' Iron Eyes screamed to himself. Yet the fog inside his skull was getting thicker and now his eyes were playing tricks on him. He narrowed his eyes and stared up to where the boulders rested on the top of the hill. They were moving as though alive. Iron Eyes blinked hard but it made no difference to the confused images he was looking at. The entire forest was swaying before him. Swaying like long grass in a stiff breeze.

Unwilling to admit defeat by invisible foes the bounty hunter tried to work out where they were. Then an arrow came out of the thickest glade. He felt the sudden pain as its sharp flint tip sliced across his ribs before hitting the tree.

The bounty hunter raised both his guns in response and fired them as one. Two wreathes of smoke encircled the barrels of his already smoking weapons. Now even firing his guns seemed to send lightning bolts of pain through his long, injured frame.

Summoning all his fast fading strength Iron Eyes pulled himself away from the tree. He felt the arrow rip his jacket and shirt as it tore the bloody fabric apart. At last he managed to free himself of the arrow which had pinned him to the tree, but he still had one stuck in his chest.

'This ain't good,' Iron Eyes muttered as he saw the blood squirting from around the wound. 'I'm getting killed here. Killed by snivelling varmints I ain't even seen yet.'

Somehow he started to run. Somehow his unsteady legs obeyed him even though he felt as though he were only a spit away from tangling with the grim reaper. Iron Eyes was bouncing off trees but he kept running. Arrows passed to both sides of him. Some caught the tails of his long trail coat and spun him around like a rag doll. The bounty hunter could not see anything clearly any longer. Nothing but the blurred colours that surrounded him. The fog was now a whirlpool unlike anything he had ever experienced previously.

Like a man possessed Iron Eyes defiantly blasted the Navy Colts again and again until his hammers fell on chambers empty of anything except spent brass casings.

'Gotta reload,' he snarled at himself.

He ducked and ran up the slope from where he had heard the pitiful scream come before the arrows had started to seek his hide out as well.

As he reached the first of the gigantic smooth boulders he tripped and fell on to his face. He spat out grass, then pushed his aching body up. He looked at the ground just behind his boots and gasped. Even his beclouded eyes could make out the dead outlaw he had been hunting. He rammed one of his guns into his belt, reached out and felt the blood on his fingertips.

'Reckon I'll be joining ya soon, Joe,' Iron Eyes told the corpse. 'Tell the Devil to set another place for supper.'

Iron Eyes gasped as he forced his long thin legs to stand once again. He looked all around him but saw nothing. Nothing but the mocking images his poisoned mind could not comprehend.

He had reached the boulders but he felt no safer. Somehow his shaking hands shook the spent casings from his smoking Colt and then he fumbled for fresh bullets in his deep coat pockets. He slid one bullet after another into the weapon, then snapped it shut. He cocked the hammer and licked his dry lips. The taste of blood was now filling his mouth.

How could he fend them off? He could see nothing but tormented colours washing before his bullet-coloured eyes. They could creep right up to the boulders without him even seeing them.

The memory of blindness swept over the bounty hunter.

He felt sick.

Was he going blind again? Or was this something else – something he had never experienced before? A hundred questions screamed inside his skull and he held on to the gun and wondered how long he had left before he would join all the outlaws he had sent to Hell. Then even in his clouded thoughts he recalled being told that some tribes used poison on their arrowheads. Poison which slowly killed their enemies.

A chill traced the length of the emaciated man.

How long did he have?

Death had ridden with the lean man all of his days but now Iron Eyes could feel the breathing on his neck. Was it finally his time to die with his boots on?

Resting his shoulder against the smooth surface of the boulder the wounded man feverishly rubbed his eyes with his free hand. Tried to rid them of the sickening haze which grew worse with every passing beat of his thundering heart.

'Gotta try and kill every last one of them varmints,' he told himself as he thought about poisoned arrows once more. 'Reckon they already done killed me.'

FOUR

The sound of the bullwhip being cracked in the hot midday streets of San Angelo was accompanied by the wailing of the small female who wielded its impressive length of plaited rawhide as she drove the stagecoach into the remote settlement. Clouds of dust curled up off its team's hoofs and the metal wheel rims as the stage careered along the town's twisting streets at breakneck pace. Startled men and women took terrified refuge in every available doorway as the stagecoach thundered into the very innards of the town. A town still stained by the mysterious bounty hunter's bloody handiwork.

A sickening smell hung on the dry afternoon air as the stagecoach raced through the streets. It was the lingering stench of rotted flesh which had refused to be washed away from the interior of the fast-moving vehicle. For every eye which stared at the unusual sight of the small female standing in the driver's box, a myriad flies followed its nauseating aroma.

The whip cracked again and again above the heads of the six muscular horses. The team were wide-eyed and chomping on their bits as they vainly attempted to flee their determined mistress.

San Angelo had not recovered from the fleeting but memorable sight of Iron Eyes the previous night. Now, a few minutes after noon, and the senses of the townsfolk were being treated to something even more unforgettable. None of the startled onlookers could believe their eyes as they stared at the young female balancing in the driver's box with whip in one hand and reins in the other. It was a sight which, like the acrid stench that accompanied it, would linger in all of their memories for a long while.

The blazing sun burned down upon the remote border town and was getting hotter the higher it rose into the cloudless sky, yet none of the townspeople seemed to notice. All they could do was watch open-mouthed as the stagecoach careened on two wheels as it rounded a corner and headed even deeper into the heart of San Angelo. The townsfolk knew that this was not one of the regular stagecoaches that visited San Angelo each day. This was the mere shell of what had once been a pristine vehicle. This horse-drawn conveyance looked as though it had been to Hell and back.

As the coach continued on even more dust rose up from its battered shell. Bits of wooden trim flew off and littered the stagecoach's route as the feisty female driver pressed on.

Squirrel Sally Cooke was on a mission and that mission was to find the deadly Iron Eyes. The six-horse team were labouring as they turned a corner and dragged their hefty cargo into the long meandering main street. Riders in the normally quiet street spurred hard and fast just to get out of the way of the relentless stage and its snorting horses. Nothing was safe as the tiny Squirrel Sally doggedly guided the vehicle towards its ultimate destination: the sheriff's office. Men and beasts alike had to leap out of the way as the snorting team towed the rocking vehicle down the long street.

As the stagecoach closed in on the empty sheriff's office the fearless young girl tossed the whip over her shoulder, then pulled back on the reins as her bare right foot pressed down on the long brake pole. The half-dead horses came to a halt outside the sheriff's office as their mistress looped the long leathers around the pole and then sat down.

A wide smile etched itself acoss her dusty face as she pulled out a corncob pipe and rammed it between her teeth.

She was as filthy as the vehicle itself, but did not seem either to mind or care. She had done what she had set out to do: get to San Angelo in one piece. She struck a match across her weathered pants leg, held its flame above the pipe bowl and sucked.

Smoke billowed from her mouth as she tossed the match away and rested her elbows on the metal

48

luggage rail. Her keen eyes watched the startled people gathering on the boardwalks on both sides of the street. She gave a grunting laugh. They posed no threat to Squirrel Sally. She blew out a line of smoke, then produced a half-consumed bottle of whiskey from the box at her feet.

As men moved closer to where the stagecoach had come to rest she pulled the bottle's cork and spat it at the team of horses beneath her high vantage point. She then raised the bottle to her lips and took a long swallow before lowering it. She dried her mouth on her sleeve and puffed on her pipe again.

Squirrel Sally was drawing people the way the inside of the coach was drawing flies. Curious folks were always drawn to curiosities and she knew it.

The stench coming from the inside of the stage was hard to handle unless your nostrils were filled with pipe-tobacco smoke and trail dust, as hers were. Most men and women held their hands to their noses as they quietly edged closer.

The decomposing bodies might have long gone but not the fragrance of death. It was still powerful, yet Squirrel Sally did not seem to notice it.

She stared at the sheriff's office and shouted. 'Sheriff.'

One of the bravest of the town's men, dressed in fancy clothes more suited to a riverboat gambler cleared his throat and moved to stand beneath the high driver's seat. He began to speak.

'What in tarnation is this?' he asked.

Sally glanced down at him with unblinking dust-caked eyes.

'Ya talking to me, handsome?'

He drew both his shoes together and raised a hand. His finger shook with every word that passed his lips.

'I am. Don't ya know that this stagecoach ya sitting on should not be here, young lady? This is an Overland Stage company vehicle and San Angelo is on the Wells Fargo route.'

'This is my stage,' she snarled as her small hand found the handle of the bullwhip again and eased it over her tight-fitting shirt.

'What?' the man asked.

'I done bought this stage. Hard cash,' Squirrel Sally told him as she returned the bottle to her mouth and took another swig. 'It goes anywhere I damn well aims it, mister. Savvy?'

More men gathered closer to the irate man.

He spoke again. 'I'm Ben Calter. I happen to be mayor of this town and I could have ya arrested. Savvy?'

Squirrel Sally removed the pipe from her mouth and pointed at the sheriff's office. Its door was still open and the lamps of the previous night still burned.

'Ya better find ya sheriff first, Ben boy,' she said, pointing her pipe at the office. 'Seems to me that ya ain't got no lawman at the moment, otherwise he'd

50

have blown them lamps out at sunup.'

Calter looked even more irate. 'I've a feeling ya stole this stagecoach. How could a young gal like you buy a stagecoach? Where'd ya get that kinda money?'

Her expression hardened. She raised the whip and swung it above the heads of the nearest men. A jerk of her hand made the leather tip crack as loudly as a pistol shot. Every person on the board-walk ducked.

'The money come from dead 'uns,' Squirrel Sally said. She tossed the whip back on the top of the coach behind her. The embarrassed men looked at one another.

'Dead 'uns?' the mayor repeated as his imagina-tion started to fire up. 'What does that mean, exactly?'

'I'm a bounty hunter,' Squirrel Sally exaggerated. 'Me and my man killed us a whole heap of outlaws and he give me the reward money. I still got me a whole heap of money left.'

'Why would ya man give you all of the reward money?' another man called out nervously from the safety of an open storefront doorway.

'He loves me, that's why.' Sally sighed. 'Iron Eyes and me are betrothed to be married. He'd give me anything I done wanted if I just asked.'

There was a hushed silence as men kept staring up at the female who appeared more confident than any of them. The mayor rubbed his freshly shaved face.

'Iron Eyes?'

'Yep.' Sally nodded. 'That's why I'm here. I come looking for the dumb critter. Reckoned if anyone knew where he is it'd be the sheriff. Where is that damn sheriff, anyways?'

'He's lying yonder in the doc's,' a voice replied. 'Half-dead by all accounts.'

Sally sucked on the stem of her pipe.

'Hold on a cotton-picking minute there. If ya betrothed to Iron Eyes how come ya weren't here with him yesterday when he done all that killing?' Calter wagged his finger again and added a few nods of his head. 'He didn't look like he was the marrying kind.'

Her eyes widened in excitement. 'So he's here? I done caught up with him at last?'

Every one of them shook their heads.

'Nope,' one answered.

'He lit out after a drifter last night,' another added.

'He killed three bank robbers before he went,' Ben Calter said, and nodded.

'Did he get paid?' Squirrel Sally asked.

The crowd all shook their heads at the same time.

'The sheriff got shot,' Calter told her. 'Iron Eyes didn't want to hang around waiting for the sheriff to recover so he rode out after another outlaw.'

'Damn it all.' Sally exhaled and then took another long swallow of the fiery liquor. She rubbed her chin and thought about the infamous Iron Eyes. She knew that the bounty hunter had locked her up in a jail cell back at Cooperville a few days earlier and had then ridden out. He had been willing to let her have the reward money on all the outlaws they had killed. Her youthful, naïve mind wondered why. Why had he ridden out without her and why had he let her have all of the bounty? 'I'm gonna kill him when I catches up with him.' She smouldered angrily. 'It just ain't right, making me trail after him.'

'I thought ya said ya was gonna get married?' a man in a straw hat asked. 'Seems mighty funny that ya gotta chase the varmint all over if'n ya getting hitched.'

Calter raised an eyebrow. 'Seems to me Iron Eyes is trying to keep one step ahead of ya, girlie.'

Squirrel Sally narrowed her eyes as her nostrils flared. 'Ya figure?'

The crowd began to mumble.

'Hush up,' Squirrel Sally demanded.

The men started to smile, and then she could hear laughter coming from them. There was fire in her eyes. A furious fire she had never been able to control.

'I got me a thought that Iron Eyes don't want nothing to do with ya, missy,' Calter said. He burst into loud roars of laughter. 'I sure don't blame him none.'

Faster than any of the men would have imagined

possible Squirrel Sally plucked her Winchester up from the driver's box. She cocked its mechanism, then started blasting. She had taken the Stetsons off three cowboy's heads before she rammed the long smoking barrel into Calter's mouth.

'Suck on this, ya slick bastard,' Sally growled as she saw the blood trailing down the faces of the trio of hatless men. 'Suck on it like it was a candy cane.'

Calter stopped laughing and started coughing.

Sally looked at the crowd with darting eyes. 'Keep making fun of me and ya gonna have to elect a new mayor, coz this 'un is gonna be dead.'

They all stopped laughing.

'Gimme a reason why I don't blow ya head clean off ya fancy shoulders, Benny boy?' she snarled. 'And don't give me no eyewash about ya being the mayor. Mayors die just as easy as any other folks. All I gotta do is tug on this trigger and every damn man and woman in this street will see I'm right.'

The mayor's tearful eyes looked to both sides. His companions were edging away from him. He gulped and tasted the gunsmoke.

'Me being a country gal, I'm kinda touchy when it comes to town folks joshing with me.' Sally pulled the rifle barrel out of his mouth. 'Makes me want to kill. I'm damn good at killing, just like my Iron Eyes. I can shoot the eye out of a buzzard's head at a hundred paces. Ya reckon ya want to die, mister?'

The mayor was now standing alone. All of the other men were at least ten feet away from him.

Most knew blood seldom splattered that far from a critter when its head was blown off.

'I . . . I apologize,' he croaked. 'I was being foolish. I was being cruel.'

She nodded in agreement and cocked the rifle again. 'Ya sure was, Benny. Where I comes from folks die for being thataway.'

The mayor mopped his brow. 'I should never have doubted that ya was a bounty hunter. I never seen anyone as fast with a carbine as you. Never.'

She straightened up. 'I'm damn accurate as well.'

Without warning she raised the rifle to her shoulder, aimed and then fired up the street. The startled audience watched as the minute hand of the church clock was shot off the building's steeple.

The crowd backed even further away as they watched the barrel suddenly return to the face of Ben Calter. Sweat trailed down his face as he stared along its length into the dusty face of the unusual girl.

'Please don't shoot me, Squirrel Sally,' Calter begged quietly as he had never begged before.

'Quit fretting. Squirrel Sally don't waste lead.' Squirrel Sally smiled as she gripped the pipe-stem in her teeth. 'Not unless I'm real riled up, that is.'

'Ain't ya riled up now?' the mayor asked fearfully.

'Just a tad.' She winked.

'Tell me. What do ya want, Squirrel Sally?' Calter stammered. 'How can we help ya?'

Sally cranked the hand guard again. A brass

casing flew over her shoulder as she stroked the mayor's cheek with the still hot barrel.

'I want me a fresh team, a few bottles of whiskey and some vittles, Benny boy.' She pulled out a leather moneybag from her shirt, poked in two fingers and withdrew some coins. She tossed a handful of them on to the boardwalk. 'And I wants me one other thing.'

Calter swallowed hard. 'What?'

Sucking on her pipe Squirrel Sally stared up the street to where the town ended and the distant forest could be viewed, bathed in golden sunlight.

'Tell me which damn way my Iron Eyes went.'

FIVE

Squirrel Sally looked even smaller when she was on the ground toting her Winchester over her shoulder and striding towards the general store. Yet, however diminutive she actually was, there was no doubting that in spirit Squirrel Sally was a giant. Few females had the power or innocent resolve to bring grown men to heel. She feared nothing and it showed. Finishing the last few drops of the whiskey she paused and glared at the scores of people who were filling the boardwalk before her. She tossed the empty bottle into the nearest trough, then pulled the rifle down until it rested in her small capable hands.

With steely resolve she forced the rifle's hand-guard swiftly down, then pulled it back up. A spent brass casing flew from the rifle magazine and followed the bottle into the water-filled trough.

Sally smiled. It was not the warm smile of friendship but the cold smile of someone who was silently warning people to get out of her way or pay the price.

The crowd duly parted and allowed her to walk up the wooden steps to the open double doors of the store. For a brief few beats of her young heart Sally paused and stared out over her shoulder. The men she had paid were unhitching her spent team of horses and leading them away. She knew it would take another few minutes before a fresh six horses were brought from the livery to replace them between the stagecoach's traces.

Sally returned her attention to the alluring and colourful emporium before her. She had never seen anything like it before. It dazzled her senses with all of its brilliance. Her small bare feet shuffled towards its wide-open doors without her even realizing that she was being lured like a fish to a well-disguised hook.

Only one man stood in the large impressive store and he was only there because he owned the place. Harvey Stutt was sixty and well rounded. What remained of his hair was as white as snow. The closer the small female got to him as he stood in the very centre of the store the redder his plump face became.

Staring at the rifle-toting barefooted female clad in rags, Stutt became wary. Like every other person in San Angelo he had never before seen anyone like his new customer. However, for all his nervousness, the sound of the coins in the leather bag which dangled from a string belt around her slim waist persuaded Stutt to be brave.

Reluctantly he moved forward as she held the rifle in her hands and glanced curiously around his stacked shelves and counters. No pirates' treasure could have been more breathtaking to the eyes of a innocent girl.

'Howdy, young lady,' Stutt heard himself say as he tried to remain calm. He kept thinking about the moneybag and its contents. 'And how can I help you?'

For a few moments Squirrel Sally said nothing. She kept looking at all his colourful wares in stunned amazement. Stutt did not know it but she had never entered a general store before and was unable to comprehend all the things he had for sale.

He cleared his throat, then caught sight of the scores of people looking through his large store windows. He tried to sweep them away with gestures of his hands but they remained glued to both windows. Stutt turned and clasped his sweating hands together.

'And what is it ya looking to buy, young lady?' He tried again to get her attention. 'As ya can see we have a good selection of wares in stock and everything you see is for sale.'

Sally exhaled quietly and then looked at the rotund figure beside her. She had never seen a man with such a wide girth before. Growing up on a ranch she had only seen lean men and women. Hard work never allowed people to grow fat.

'Ya got any trail gear?' she asked.

'I sure have.' Stutt walked to a counter filled with stacks of breeches and shirts of every known colour. He patted one of the piles. 'Take a look at these.'

She looked and then nodded.

'Mighty bright. I never seen such pretty colours.'

'They sure are pretty, young lady,' Stutt agreed. 'And mighty hard-wearing. These shirts and pants are held together with metal rivets just like the kind goldminers wear over in California.'

Squirrel Sally gave a shrug. 'Hell! I ain't going goldmining, old-timer. I'm gonna be sitting atop my stagecoach whipping a team of nags.'

The curious crowd were watching everything that was going on inside the general store. Stutt turned his back on the faces pressed up against his windows and forced a smile. 'What I'm trying to say is that these clothes are tough. Tough enough to withstand anything.'

'That's what I'm looking for.' Sally turned and patted her backside before she pulled at the shining material to reveal her pink flesh. A split beside the seam of the weathered fabric went from just below the belt line to somewhere around her crotch. 'I sure feels the draught down here.'

'Ah, yes. I see ya problem.' Stutt moved between Sally and the uninvited voyeurs before any of them saw what he had just seen. 'I've got lots of pants for ya to choose from.'

The young female looked at her worn clothes. They were stained with blood and ripped by all the events which she had endured over the previous couple of weeks since she had first encountered Iron Eyes.

'These are kinda weathered,' she observed, pulling at the frail fabric of what had once been a shirt. The material tore like wet paper in her clumsy fingers, revealing one of her small breasts to the already embarrassed man. 'Ya see I bin a tad busy killing outlaws and the like. Me and my betrothed Iron Eyes, got ourselves roughed up real bad tackling them varmints. Reckon my clothes are just tuckered.'

Stutt nodded as all good businessmen nod when they sense a sale pending. 'I fully understand, young lady. There is only so much wear and tear even good clothing can take before it gets really worn out. I guess killing outlaws can be pretty hard on clothes.'

'Ya dead right there.' Squirrel Sally lifted a red shirt and smiled. 'Blood sure rots breeches fast if'n it goes dry before ya can scrub it off.'

Stutt nodded. 'Yeah. Guess it does.'

'I sure do like this 'un.' Squirrel Sally sighed as she looked at the well-made shirt. 'It's real pretty.'

'Ya so right. Red is a very flattering colour, young lady.' Stutt sighed.

'And it don't show the bloodstains as easy as

most,' she added drily.

Harvey Stutt swallowed nervously. 'Exactly.'

'Ya got any britches the same colour?' she asked eagerly.

Stutt shook his head. 'Only got blue and brown pants. Most times it's only men that buy 'em. They don't like wearing anything too bright.'

'That's a damn shame, old-timer. Reckon I'll just have to take me some brown breeches then.' Sally lifted a pair of pants and allowed them to unroll. They were for someone with much longer legs. 'Leastways, brown won't show the mud. I tend to spend a lotta time rolling in the mud. Shoot-outs can get damn dirty when ya trapped behind a trough chewing on gunsmoke and eating dirt.'

The large man blinked hard and tried to understand the way this small young female reasoned. It was not easy. He looked at the pants in her hands and the foot of material on the floor in front of her feet.

'Those are far too long for such small legs as you have, dear lady.' Stutt smiled and pulled a tape-measure from round his neck and knelt down. 'I'll measure ya legs so we can find the right size for ya.'

As the tape was placed next to her groin and allowed to unravel down to her ankle Stutt felt the rifle rest on his shoulder. Nervously he looked into her face. She was looking at him with furious eyes.

'And what in tarnation do ya think ya doing down there, old-timer?' she hissed. 'I heard about old critters like you trying to get their wicked way with innocent gals like me. I do happen to be spoken for, ya know.'

Sweat rolled down his face. Stutt gulped and watched her finger curl around the weapon's trigger. 'Ya got the wrong idea. I . . . I'm just measuring ya leg length, young lady.'

'Can't ya just guess?'

The old man jumped back to his feet and threw the tape away and nodded firmly. 'I surely can. I'm the town's best man at guessing.'

'Good.' Sally sniffed and then rested her Winchester against the side of the counter. 'I don't want to have me no babies, ya know.'

'Babies?' Frantically Stutt searched the pile of pants and then found a pair that seemed about right. He thrust them into her hands. 'There.'

She looked at the shirt and the pants and nodded. 'I reckon these look fine. I sure hope they don't itch.'

'Have no fears.' Stutt smiled. 'My clothing is of the softest cotton ya can buy.'

Squirrel Sally said nothing as she carefully rested the shirt and pants down on the edge of the counter. Then she held on to the bottom of her frayed shirt and pulled it apart. What few buttons were left went flying across the boarded floor of the store as she removed her shirt and tossed it away, revealing her petite naked upper half.

'W-what ya doing?' Stutt stammered, trying to

hide her from the eyes of those who were still peering into his store through his large windows.

'I ain't never bought me no new clothes before.' Squirrel Sally said innocently. She then unbuttoned her well-soiled pants and forced them down off her pink flesh. The frail material fell to bits before she had completed her undressing. 'There sure is one hell of a draught in here, old-timer.'

Harvey Stutt heard the watching crowd gasp in both horror and lustful amusement at the sight of the naked young female. He tried to shield her from their prying eyes but even he was not wide enough to achieve his goal. His heart was pounding inside his chest as he looked at her slim attractive form. His eyes widened and he felt himself stagger as though he were about to faint.

'Ya ain't meant to strip off in here,' he blurted.

Shaking the shirt and pants Squirrel Sally looked at him curiously. 'Then how am I gonna get my new trail gear on if'n I don't take the old 'uns off? Ya sure talks real dumb for a grown-up old man.'

Frantically Stutt waved his hands at a curtain at the rear of the store. 'There. Over there. That's the changing area. Not here for all to see.'

By the time he had stopped ranting she had dressed in her new pants and shirt. Sally nodded as she looked down at her clean clothes. The first new clothes she had ever owned. Only her dirty feet spoiled the full effect of the transformation.

'I gotta remember to wash my feet some time,'

she noted to herself.

'I sell shoes.' Stutt gestured to a wall filled with boxes of various types of shoes and boots.

'I don't like shoes.' She sniffed. 'They slow ya up when ya trying to outrun a bullet.'

Stutt shrugged. 'I guess they do.'

'I look kinda good though.'

The flustered man sat down on a chair and cupped his red face in his hands. 'Yep. Ya look wonderful, young lady. Even better with clothes on.'

She handed the man some silver dollars, picked up her rifle again and stared out into the street as men hitched up a fresh six-horse team to her stagecoach.

'Reckon I'll be going, old-timer,' Sally said as she walked out to the sun-baked street. 'Thank ya kindly for all ya help, except the bit when ya touched me down yonder. So long.'

Harvey Stutt raised a hand and feebly waved. 'So long.'

SIX

Even though his eyes were still playing tricks on him and refusing to obey the simple command of seeing, Iron Eyes knew that at least an hour had passed since he had taken refuge beside the mighty rocks. The sun was now over his shoulder and he could feel its heat on the side of his scarred face. The Indians had seemingly vanished from the hillside but he knew they were still close. He could still smell their scent on the gentle breeze that moved between the boulders. They were still there and now he sensed that they had surrounded him.

His bony hands clutched the pair of Navy Colts tightly but he doubted that he could hit any of them before they overwhelmed him.

They were playing cat and mouse with the wounded bounty hunter and he was the mouse.

The swirling haze had not got any worse since he had found the sanctuary of the smooth boulders, yet it was getting no better. He had managed to

stem the flow of blood for the time being by remaining like a statue against the smooth rock. Yet he
knew that the pool of gore which surrounded his
boots was proof that he could not afford to lose
much more.

He raised one of his guns and tried to focus along
its sights but failed. His eyes had failed him before
but this was different, he thought. This was very different. The blurred shapes and colours mocked his
every attempt to see the braves who had put the
arrow into him earlier.

He blinked hard but it was useless.

'Work, damn it!' Iron Eyes growled. Again he
lowered the pistol until it rested against his blood-
soaked pants leg. 'This ain't like before. How come
I can't see nothing but damn fog?'

The question had repeated itself a thousand
times inside his head since he had felt the sickening
haze overwhelm him. Then he realized that the
arrowhead might have been tipped, not with a
deadly poison, but something else. Something
which confused and made its victim helpless to
defend himself.

Could that be it?

Had he been drugged?

If so, why? Why were the Indians trying to make
his mind and eyes play tricks on him? Why were
they not simply killing him?

There was no sense in that.

Or was there?

67

Maybe they wanted him alive, he considered. But they had made short work of Joe Kane. None of it made any sense. Wearily Iron Eyes dropped one of the guns into his deep trail-coat pockets and then poked the other into his belt. His long thin fingers pressed into his eyes, then he felt his legs start to weaken.

'I lost too much blood,' he mumbled as he defied his body and refused to fall. 'I ain't gonna make it out of this mess. Not alive anyway.'

Then, for the first time for nearly an hour he heard noise. The noise of feet running through grass. He pushed his lean frame away from the boulder and tried to work out where the sound was coming from.

It was impossible.

The sound was coming from all around the rocks.

They were all around him.

His hand had gone for the gun tucked into his belt when he caught a glimpse of something flying through the array of colours which faced him. Before his mind had time to work out what it was hurtling in his direction he felt something smash into the side of his face. As the projectile bounced off his scarred features Iron Eyes caught it.

Unlike most of the tomahawks he had seen in recent times this one was crude. There was no metal axehead. This one was a tomahawk fashioned from a wooden shaft, lashed leather and a smooth rock.

It was designed to stun, not to kill.

It had done its job perfectly. Iron Eyes staggered backwards and then fell.

Agonizing pain ripped though his back as he landed on the arrowhead protruding from his back. By the time his screams left his mouth they were upon him like a platoon of army ants.

It felt as though warm water was washing over his hideous features but, even dazed by the powerful impact, the bounty hunter knew that it was not water that was flowing from the massive gash in his face.

It was blood.

There were a score of them. Each painted face stared down at the man with one of their arrows protruding from his chest. Iron Eyes tried to raise the gun and tomahawk high enough for him to start killing, but it was useless.

He was simply too weak.

The Indians tore his weaponry from him and then rested their feet on his wrists and ankles. More pain ripped through his tormented frame as he vainly wriggled.

'Get off me, ya bastards.'

They did not obey.

He was their prisoner.

His mind raced. How many times he had encountered other Indians of various tribes in his long journey from childhood to where he now lay?

Why was it that all any of them ever wanted to do was kill him? What was it about him that seemed to make every tribe of Indians he ever bumped into want to kill Iron Eyes?

'Why don't ya damn well kill me then?' Iron Eyes heard himself yell out. 'What ya waiting for?'

Delirium washed over the man lying helplessly on the ground at their feet. He tried to raise his head but then a moccasin pushed his bleeding face back down.

Iron Eyes blinked hard but his eyes still refused to obey. He saw nothing but swirling vapours.

'Give me my guns back, ya galoots,' he snarled. 'I'll kill the whole bunch of ya.'

Once more the mysterious Indians ignored his rantings. Iron Eyes swung his head back and forth until his eyes briefly cleared and permitted him to see his foes for the first time.

He did not recognize them.

They were of a tribe he had never encountered before.

Iron Eyes felt himself being lifted up. He struggled but it made no difference. They were in total control. He was now theirs to do with as they wanted. He was being carried away deeper into the forested hills, like a trophy.

His head fell to one side. He stared through his limp black hair at the ground moving below his helpless carcass.

Where were they taking him?

And what for?

Suddenly everything went dark. Iron Eyes was unconscious.

70

SEVEN

A few precious minutes before Squirrel Sally had set out from San Angelo a desperate Mayor Ben Calter had taken two of his gunmen with him and ridden at breakneck pace to his well-hidden ranch a few miles east of the remote settlement, just north of the wooded hills. Calter was not a man to panic easily but something had disturbed the well-dressed politician and forced him into action.

It was the name of the notorious bounty hunter: Iron Eyes.

For, contrary to the peaceful, stammering, law-abiding mayor that Calter pretended to be, he was actually a man with a secret. He now feared that at long last it might be discovered.

Just like all those whom the infamous Iron Eyes hunted, Calter was wanted dead or alive himself.

There was nothing genuine about Ben Calter.

Not even his name.

He had stolen the name from a marker he had

once seen on a boot hill a few hundred miles to the north of San Angelo, when Rafe Bond had been trying to outride a dogged posse that just would not let up. Wanted outlaw Rafe Bond had become Ben Calter and his fortunes had blossomed.

It had proved to be a profitable handle.

Within a mere few months of arriving in the border town the well-attired Ben Calter had risen to the respectable position of mayor of San Angelo. The sudden improvement in his fortunes had nothing to do with luck or popularity, though. Nothing to do with honesty. At heart Rafe Bond was still an outlaw even with his change of name and image. He had quickly realized that the small remote town was perfectly situated for his brand of criminal endeavour.

San Angelo had welcomed him because when he arrived he had brought much-needed money. Enough money to buy votes and with it a certain mark of loyalty. Poor people know that sometimes it pays to turn a blind eye to the activities of men who happen to put food in the bellies of your offspring.

Calter might have looked like a riverboat dandy, but nothing could have been further from the truth. With Calter nothing was what it seemed to be. His stammering when faced with Squirrel Sally had been a well-rehearsed act. One which he had used many times in order to get the advantage over someone he wanted to best.

Calter had quickly realized that if Sally were

actually the betrothed of the infamous bounty hunter Iron Eyes, as she claimed to be, it was wise to give her anything she wanted in order to keep the bounty hunter out of San Angelo. For men like Iron Eyes have the images of all wanted men branded into their very hides and Calter could not risk being recognized.

Calter had managed to avoid encountering the bounty hunter when he had been in town killing the Lucas gang, and he had sighed with relief when he had been told that Iron Eyes had ridden after the ill-fated Joe Kane.

Even though Joe Kane had only been in town the previous evening because Calter had sent for him, Kane's fate meant nothing to him. The mayor had wanted Kane to add to his small army of hardened outlaws on his payroll: outlaws whom he hid in his ranch on the outskirts of San Angelo. There were already a score of other outlaws working for Calter. Each was well paid for doing his bidding on both sides of the border. It had become a very well-oiled operation: mining silver in Mexico and then shipping it north for a vast profit.

Yet Ben Calter knew only too well that even the smoothest of operations can fall foul of men like Iron Eyes. Men who live their lives by hunting down outlaws wanted dead or alive for the bounty on their heads.

Calter had no desire for that fate to befall him.

The three horsemen had thundered away from

San Angelo towards the ranch Ben Calter had pur-
chased as a place where his hired gunmen could
take refuge. As they had ridden Calter reflected that
the seemingly unimportant forested hills to their
right were in fact the key to his fortune.

For the wooded hills were spread over the
unmarked border which separated Texas from
Mexico. A myriad trees gave a lot of cover to those
who had illegally carved a trail through the once
pristine forest.

The fact that the forest was designated Indian territory and it was forbidden for any white man to
enter unless invited meant nothing to the lead rider
as he spurred hard and rode on to his ranch. For
just as he used his wealth to control the inhabitants
of San Angelo, Calter had found another way to
control the Indians.

A far more brutal and bloody way.

The rocking stagecoach had made good progress
along the well-worn dusty road from San Angelo to
where the parched ground gave way to the foothills
of the tree-covered hills beyond. Squirrel Sally had
decided not to ride up on the driver's box but to sit
astride the lead horse of the fresh team so that she
was able to keep an eye out for the distinctive hoof-
tracks of Iron Eyes's mighty stallion. Tracks she
knew like the back of her hand.

The chains of the harness livery rattled out a
sorrowful tune along the traces behind her as the

74

six horses obeyed their new mistress. Gripping the sides of the blinkered horse between her strong thighs the small female held on to its mane and urged it on until something ahead caught her eagle-eyed attention.

Powerfully Sally pulled back on the black mane of the horse beneath her until the team and coach came to a reluctant halt.

Dust curled upwards into the cloudless blue sky as the feisty Sally surveyed the ground with the attention of a hungry bird of prey. Nothing escaped her keen eyes even though the road was well used mostly by stagecoaches. She knew exactly what she was looking for and a million other tracks on the carved up road could not hide the truth from her hunter's soul. For, like her beloved Iron Eyes, she was a hunter. A hunter of all creatures both two- and four-legged.

Nothing escaped her.

Countless wheel-rim grooves and hoofmarks were cut into the yellow sand but she saw none of them. Her eyes burned down at something else.

All tracks tell a story to those capable of reading them and she was more than capable. Broken brush to the side of the road had been the first thing she had spotted. That told her that a rider had left the road and cut across the range towards the wall of trees. Squirrel Sally was looking for the familiar hoofmarks of the powerful palomino stallion that the bounty hunter rode. Weeks earlier she had noticed one of the horse's hoofs had a distinctive crack in it.

Once she spotted a hoof mark with a crack in it she would know for certain that she had found the trail left by Iron Eyes.

A smile etched itself across her pretty face. Faster than spit she threw her leg over the head of the snorting horse and dismounted. Her small bare feet raced across the baking-hot sand until she reached the spot where the road ended and the untamed terrain began. She felt the hairs on her neck rise beneath her tied-back ponytail as she leaned over and surveyed the ground close to the broken brush.

The cracked hoofmark was there. She had found it.

'Got ya.' She grinned and bit her lower lip. 'I'll learn ya not to lock ya loved one up in no jail cell, Iron Eyes.'

She aimed a finger at the shimmering heat haze and worked out where the horse had gone after it had left the road. Sally had assumed that the bounty hunter and his prey would stay on the well-furrowed road but the broken brush told a different tale.

'That outlaw must have been mighty scared to head off in that direction, Iron Eyes,' Sally muttered to herself, as though the bounty hunter could actually hear her every word. 'Mind you, I reckon most folks would be a tad scared if'n they caught sight of you on their tail.'

The youthful lass reached out and took hold of

one of the broken shafts of wild grass. It had been snapped at stirrup height during the night. She could tell by its now browning tip that the sun was burning the frost off its damaged stem. She squinted out over the wild range once more to where she knew both horsemen had gone.

'Them boys was headed for that damn forest OK,' Sally said, rubbing her face thoughtfully. 'I bet Iron Eyes killed that varmint before he even reached there. Yep. I bet I'll bump into the skinny critter before I even gets halfway to them trees.'

Sally nodded to herself and then focused hard on the distant forest. Her eyes searched in vain for any sign of the bounty hunter returning with his prey. 'Then how come I don't see ya headed back here, Iron Eyes?'

A troubled Squirrel Sally scratched her neck, then walked back to the team of waiting horses. She made her way to the smaller wheel on the driver's side and climbed up to the box. Then she untied the six lengths of heavy reins, which she had secured earlier. Her bare right foot pushed the brake pole forward until she had it gripped by her toes. Once more her attention went to the countless trees a couple of miles away from the road.

She sighed and felt troubled, but then dismissed her fears and concentrated. 'Iron Eyes sure is hard to court. Now, I wonder if'n I can get this damn coach up through there? No matter. I'll give it a damn good try.'

She allowed the brake pole to spring back, then whipped the reins across the backs of the six horses and carefully steered the long vehicle off the road and across the wilder, less predictable ground.

'I'm coming, sweetheart,' she hollered out at the top of her voice. 'Coming for them sweet kisses ya ain't given me yet. Reckon ya must be hankering for me by now. I got me some new clothes, Iron Eyes. Real pretty clothes. Ya best like 'em or I'll have to shoot ya again.'

The stagecoach rolled on through the increasingly high grass and brush towards the wall of trees which seemed to go on for ever in both directions.

As the terrain grew more inhospitable Sally began to sense that the man she sought so desperately was close. Her eyes narrowed as she brought the reins down on the backs of the team of steaming horses beneath her high perch and forced them on.

He was in there somewhere, she reasoned. Iron Eyes was in the forest. She lashed the reins down hard. The brush was broken ahead of her where two horses had ploughed a direct route towards the darkness of the forested hills.

Her hunting instincts were telling her to keep going.

Iron Eyes was ahead of her somewhere amid the great mass of trees, probably blowing the smoke from his gun barrels as he hauled another dead outlaw off the ground and threw him over the cantle of his saddle.

That was it, she kept telling herself.

Iron Eyes was up there rubbing the blood off his hands and grunting in satisfaction. He had probably let the outlaw run just for the hell of it.

That was it.

The trees were like a barrier built by a military expert. There seemed to be little sign of where the two horsemen had entered the woodland. She slowed the team by leaning back and pressing the brake pole with her small foot.

The stagecoach ground to a halt beneath her. Squirrel Sally looked to both sides and then snorted almost as loudly as any of the horses she controlled.

She pulled the cork of her whiskey bottle and held it out, as though its aroma might find its way to the bounty hunter's flared nostrils.

'I got me whiskey, boy,' she yelled before taking a swig and replacing the cork in the bottle's neck. She placed the bottle down and picked up her corncob pipe.

The stem was thrust between her teeth as she brooded and kept searching for a way into the wood, wide enough for her to drive her team and coach through.

There was none.

She struck a match along the side of her pants and sucked in the smoke from her freshly primed pipe. Wreaths of grey smoke billowed from the mouth of the frustrated youngster.

'Damn it all,' Sally muttered as she looked at the broken branches straight ahead of her horses. 'Iron Eyes must have forgot that I got me this stage to trail him. There ain't much room through that brush for his horse, let alone nothing else. How did he figure I was gonna be able to follow him through there?'

With smoke clouds rising from above her head she released the brake pole and encouraged the horses to retrace their steps backwards. The terrified team did exactly as their new mistress wanted and all carefully eased themselves back away from the trees.

Squirrel Sally stopped her team, then gave the wider view of the obstacle a few moments' considered thought. About a half-mile to her left the ground dipped. At first she did not even notice this until she spied a deer running from the cover of the high grass towards the trees.

She instinctively snatched her rifle up and cranked its mechanism. A brass casing flew over her arm as she watched the animal vanish from sight for a few seconds before reappearing.

Sally lowered the rifle barrel, pulled the pipe-stem from her mouth and spat a lump of brown goo at the ground.

'Must be something over there I ain't figured,' she told herself. 'Might be a road. A road that'll let me drive up into this damn thicket.'

Knowing that it would take far too long for her to turn the coach round she held on to her

Winchester and stuffed her pockets with bullets from the cartridge box next to her hip. She jumped down to the ground, and walked towards the spot where she had sighted the deer.

As she reached the exact place where the deer had disappeared from sight she suddenly knew why.

There was a road.

A crude, dirt-track road barely wider than one wagon, that led from the main road behind her and went up into the tree-covered hills.

Sally stepped down on to the rough track, then knelt as her eyes studied the brown surface of the well-hidden road.

She stood back up and nodded to herself.

'Somebody bin using this track quite a bit lately by my reckoning,' she told herself. 'The weeds ain't had time to regrow since the last wagon used it.'

The young female was curious.

Who would carve out a track which led up into the heart of a wooded hillside and why? The question burned like a branding-iron in her soul. For, like the man she wanted so desperately to catch up with, she disliked unanswered questions.

'Who bin using this trail?' The words had barely left her lips when she felt the ground tremble slightly under her bare feet. She swung the rifle around until it was ready for action, and then tilted her head. She listened hard. 'A wagon. A wagon and it's coming thisaway. I best take cover.'

The female threw herself back up from the road

into the high grass and brushes and then hid behind a large bush. The rifle in her hands was aimed up into the gloom of the forest, from where the sound was coming. With every second that passed the noise grew louder. She could hear the chains of the wagon's team rattling as the two horses galloped out of the forest and into the blazing afternoon sunshine.

Sally screwed up her eyes and peered through the bushes at the wagon. Two men sat on the drives board. One was the driver and the other a guard, who clutched his scattergun firmly to his chest.

Within a mere scratch of the nose the wagon had thundered past the place where Squirrel Sally was hiding. She slowly raised herself up as the wagon reached the main road and turned to the right. It then disappeared into the heat haze.

Clouds of dust wafted over the area off the dry road that the wagon had used. She rested the barrel of her Winchester against her small shoulder and again spat.

'Now ain't that curious?' she asked herself. 'A wagon with a canvas tarp over its flatbed. I sure do hanker to know what was under that canvas. Must be worth a pretty penny or why else would the driver need himself a guard? Yep. That sure is mighty interesting.'

The dust had gone and she was still pondering.

She was about to turn and walk back to the stage-coach when she heard the exact same sound again.

She dropped down on to her knees and again looked through the bushes.

Less than five minutes after the first wagon had rolled out of the forest another emerged into the sunlight. This one was virtually identical to the first: a flatbed, with its cargo hidden under a large canvas. The driver had a well-armed guard sitting at his side.

Another cloud of dust rolled over the kneeling female as she watched the wagon take exactly the same route that the first had used. Again Sally rose to her feet and scratched her chin.

'Now ain't that just tormenting?' She sighed. 'I surely do wonder what them wagons is doing.'

Then a more chilling thought overwhelmed the young woman as she walked back to where she had left the stagecoach amid the wild brush.

What if Iron Eyes had ridden into the forest and bumped into those varmints? She gulped.

Those guards looked ready for business with their scatterguns itching in their hands. Their breed shot first and never asked any questions.

What if Iron Eyes had run up against them? What if they had shot him simply for being there? He might be lying wounded or even dead somewhere in the woodland.

Her heart began to pound.

Squirrel Sally ran towards her stagecoach.

EIGHT

There was an eerie, haunting sound which somehow managed to penetrate the unconscious mind of the bounty hunter as he was carried ever deeper into the forest. It skewered its way into the deepest parts of his brain, played upon the faint, glowing embers of his fiery soul and reignited them. Iron Eyes might have been totally helpless and badly wounded but something in his spirit refused to drown in the foul miasma that had overwhelmed him.

Iron Eyes did not die easy.

Even unconscious he still fought.

The strange noise tormented the helpless Iron Eyes and slowly but surely began to draw him back from the place where only his nightmares reigned supreme. No crashing of thunderclaps could have equalled the raging battle inside his skull. It kept growing in volume until at last it snapped the bounty hunter back to partial awareness. Iron Eyes shook his head and slowly became aware that he was being carried across rugged terrain like fresh captured game.

As his confused mind began to recapture its wits he suddenly realized that he was utterly helpless. For the first time in his life he could do nothing but hang from his captors' shoulders and await his fate.

A chilling sense of reality swept through him. Iron Eyes had finally been defeated. The hunter was now the hunted. The invasive sound grew louder. It was mocking him. Mocking his inability to defend himself any longer. Mocking his incapability to fight.

The delirium which had swept over him after the flint arrowhead had found its target was now gone. Yet he could not see those who had triumphed over him, those who were carrying his bloodstained body. For a moment he feared that his blindness had returned to add to his misery. Then he realized that his eyelids were stuck firmly together with dried blood.

All he could do was hear. Hear the spine-chilling noise which had awoken him. His long thin frame hurt. Every part of him was being tortured by pain. Pain which ripped through his every fibre and sinew and refused to ease up. The mists of confusion might have evaporated but now his crystal-clear mind could feel all of the wounds his emaciated body had endured.

Once again he tried to force his eyelids to part, to

allow him to see who it was who carried him; to see where they were taking him, but it was impossible. The dried blood was like glue.

Iron Eyes felt his body being carried like a rag doll by unknown hands. Each of their steps sent daggers of pain tearing through him.

He was defenceless: hanging face down as his victors kept on making their way through the woodland. Suddenly he felt the taste of vomit in his mouth. It drained between his teeth and fell to the ground.

The sound grew even more intense.

Iron Eyes wondered how long he had been unconscious and how far they had been carrying him.

Where was he? his brain kept asking.

Where were they taking him?

Why had they not killed him as they had killed Joe Kane? Why?

He had no answers.

All Iron Eyes knew for sure was that he was still being carried like a fresh-killed deer. Once more he tried to blink as the noise grew even louder inside his pounding head. His eyelids remained stuck together and refused to part and let him see. He tried to move his hands but they were still being firmly gripped by the powerful hands of his unseen enemies.

Maybe they thought he was dead, just like Joe Kane.

His head dropped forward as the muscles in his thin neck yielded to the pain which was now racing unchecked through him. The taste of blood and vomit filled his mouth again but he had no spittle to make the taste go away.

He needed whiskey. Rotgut whiskey. A whole keg of whiskey.

Iron Eyes felt his mane of long matted hair clinging to his face as his tortured frame bounced up and down atop the shoulders of his silen bearers.

Was this the end?

The end of Iron Eyes?

His mind screamed to him to fight but there was nothing he could do but accept his fate until either his strength returned or they released their grip on him. He wondered where his trusty guns were. Had the Indians discarded them or had they brought them with them on the long painful trek through the daunting terrain?

If he had his guns he could teach them that it never pays to tangle with Iron Eyes, he told himself. It might cost him whatever was left of his life but he would fight to the last bullet.

Again he tried to open his eyes. Again he failed.

The Indians continued on towards their destination.

They were silent. Still silent. A thousand thoughts flashed through his mind as he realized that wherever they were taking him it was probably the last place on earth that any sane man wanted to go.

He was no longer the hunter.

He was the prize.

A mere trophy.

A trophy to be paraded before the children and females of the unknown tribe. He might not have any idea who they were but perhaps they, like all of the other tribes he had encountered, knew of him.

The living ghost.

The monster known as Iron Eyes. A creature who it was said, could not be killed because he was already dead.

He had seen what happened to those pitiful souls who fell prey to the torturous hands of others. How the tribes' womenfolk spit upon and whip the help-less captives as their triumphant men beat their chests before finally finishing the job.

Those who had defeated Iron Eyes would never allow any of their kind to forget how they had been the ones who brought the infamous bounty hunter into their camp. The campfires would tell the stories of their triumph for all time.

The scent of smoke filled his nostrils. The Indians camp was close now, Iron Eyes reasoned. Time was running out faster than his blood had done when the arrow had penetrated his chest. If he were to escape he had to do it now.

He tried vainly to free himself from their com-bined grasp. It was useless. He was too weak and they were far too strong.

Iron Eyes could hear the sound again. The devilish

sound which told him that death would be a mercy compared to what he had seen others endure.

He wriggled but there was no escape. They kept on carrying him towards the scent of smoke.

Iron Eyes thought about the brief glimpse he had got of the Indians before he had collapsed and passed out. He had no idea who these Indians were. They did not look like any of the other tribes he had met and fought with over the years. They did not act or dress in a way he recognized.

Maybe that was why he was still alive.

All of the Apaches he had ever fought with would have killed and gutted him by now. Even the Cheyenne would not have allowed him to remain alive this long.

A thought occurred to him.

Maybe they did not know who he was.

Maybe luck was still on his side.

Whoever these people were they defied all the rules he had grown to expect Indians to obey.

He screwed up his blood-covered face and tried to force the congealed blood to part and allow him to open his eyes. Again he failed.

At last the sound which had tormented him for so long seemed to be getting fainter. Pain racked his every sinew. Then he realized that the deafening noise which had mocked and awoken him was in fact the beating of his own heart.

For some reason it was no longer pulsating its deafening din in his ears. Maybe he had run out of blood, he thought. Hearts needed blood to make them work. Maybe all of his had drained from his wounds.

Again Iron Eyes tried to free his limbs but their combined grips were too vigorous. They were too strong for a man who had felt most of his blood dripping out of his wounded carcass.

There was no point in fighting any longer.

Iron Eyes knew when he was beaten.

It was a new experience for the bounty hunter. One he did not enjoy but now, after all the years during which he had battled his way through the Wild West, he finally had to admit that he was finished.

Death had ridden on his shoulder for so many years.

Now it was going to claim him.

Blood filled his throat and then poured from his open mouth yet his captors did not miss a step and continued to carry their prize to wherever it was they were headed.

Then Iron Eyes heard another sound.

This was not the pounding of his heart. This was the sound of drums. Drums being beaten by rows of seated warriors. Another sound grew even louder than that of the drums.

It was the wailing song of victory.

Then he heard bells. So many small bells. Iron Eyes knew that many tribes tied bells around their ankles when they danced. It was a way to arouse the

pleasure of their gods before they sacrificed something or someone.

Cold sweat trailed down over his face.

Their steps grew slower, then abruptly stopped.
He could hear the voices of excited children and
encouraging females. Then the deeper voices of
dancing warriors were all around him.

The bounty hunter was lowered down until he lay
on his face in the dirt. He felt the arrow snap under
his chest. A bolt of lightning thrust through him as
the splintered wooden shaft tormented his already
agonized wound. Then he felt the flint arrowhead
being gripped and tugged from his back.

Iron Eyes wanted to scream out but refused to
allow any sign of weakness. He gritted his teeth and
tried to remain silent.

The smell of a campfire filled his flared nostrils.
Its light managed to pass through his closed lids.

The ground under his face vibrated as dozens of
feet beat out a dance all around him. His right hand
tried to reach his face but a foot pressed down upon
his back.

Iron Eyes inhaled dirt and turned his face.

The wailing and drumming became deafening.

Defiantly Iron Eyes struggled against his agony
and forced himself up off his face until he was balancing like a whipped dog on all fours. The sound
of their celebration suddenly stopped.

Perhaps they were surprised that anyone so badly
injured could manage the feat. Whatever the

reason, it chilled him to the bone. Although he could not see them he knew that every one of the Indians was watching his valiant battle to find once more the strength to stand.

The palms of his hands pressed into the dirt. Even though he was far less heavy than most men of his height and girth Iron Eyes felt as though a full-grown buffalo was sitting on his back, forcing him to submit.

But he would never submit.

Death had to fight damn hard if it wanted to best him.

Then for the umpteenth time he tried to rid his eyes of the dried blood which had glued his lids together when suddenly he felt warm liquid hit his tortured features hard. He rocked on his knees as the mocking laughter of a lone female was soon joined by the amused sounds of others. He was soaked. His flared nostrils told him that she had not wasted precious water in the assault but another far less valuable liquid.

At least it was warm, he wearily concluded.

The dancing started again along with the wailing.

He could hear the bells on their ankles start moving around him again as the liquid ran down his hideous features. Iron Eyes knew that it had not been the female's intention but she had done him a favour. The faceful of warm liquid waste had dampened the dried gore and allowed him at last to open his eyes once again.

92

Iron Eyes blinked and swallowed hard.

For the first time for hours he was able to see clearly, yet the vision which greeted him filled him with renewed dread. This was not good, he silently told himself. His eyes darted from one group of people to another. There were at least a hundred of them and they were all chanting with the same venomous looks on their faces.

The wounded bounty hunter remained on all fours like a dog.

He was unable either to rise or fall. Iron Eyes attempted to muster another brief spurt of energy but he was too weak. His head fell forward and he stared along his blood-soaked clothing. The shattered arrow was twisted across his chest. Droplets of blood still dripped from the torn flesh and fell from the feathered flight on to the dirt beneath him.

'Damn ya all to Hell,' he growled sadly. 'Why don't ya just kill me? Kill me like ya killed Joe Kane.'

His words fell on deaf ears. None of those who surrounded him wanted to kill the thin man. Not quickly. They had a more lingering death planned for him. One which would take a lot longer than the kind of retribution he was used to dishing out for the men he hunted.

Iron Eyes always killed his prey swiftly.

Even the worst two-legged vermin were dispatched speedily on their journey to Hell. He saw no profit in torturing anyone just for the sake of it.

He shook his head. Bloody droplets flew to either side as he managed to raise his head and stare at them through the limp strands of his black mane which covered his scarred face.

Who were they?

The question kept returning as he focused on their clothing and faces. These were not the sort of Indians he was used to. They were another, totally different tribe. Then to his surprise Iron Eyes noticed his palomino stallion being held by some of the braves who had brought him to this place. Its ornate Mexican saddle and bags were on its back.

Iron Eyes did not understand. Horses were of little use to these people, he reasoned. Unless they intended eating it. He doubted if many of their tribe ever rode a horse through this forest. It was too dense. A man could move faster on foot. So why had they brought the stallion with its fallen master to their encampment?

He nodded slightly. They were going to eat it, he told himself once more. The only good horse he had ever owned was going to end up in the bellies of these Indians.

His bloodshot eyes drifted wearily to the centre of the clearing. He felt his heart quicken its pace. Set about fifteen feet away from a roaring camp-fire a sturdy wooden stake more than a foot wide was embedded securely into the red dirt. It stood over ten feet high and had been trimmed of all its

94

branches.

The stake was charred. Its bark had long since been burned from its trunk.

The stake was surrounded by dry kindling. An awful lot of dried kindling. Enough kindling to burn a man until he was nothing more than a blackened memory. He inhaled as deep as his pain would allow and narrowed his eyes.

Iron Eyes sighed.

He suddenly realized what the Indians intended doing to him.

'Damn it all,' he growled angrily. 'Reckon it ain't just my horse that's gonna get roasted here.'

The Indians were chanting feverishly. The womenfolk gave out shrills of excitement as the children began to throw stones at the helpless man on his knees.

Then somehow Iron Eyes dug deeper into his reserves of strength than he had ever done before. He forced himself off the ground in one burst of energy and hovered.

He was upright and standing with clenched fists.

The chanting faded until the encampment fell silent as they encircled him.

'Well? Ya gonna finish me or am I gonna have to kill the whole bunch of ya with my bare hands?' Iron Eyes yelled. 'C'mon. I'm waiting. What'll it be?'

Every eye stared at the defiant, blood-soaked figure.

Staring through his limp black hair the bounty

hunter saw their bows being readied with fresh arrows. He exhaled.

'I hates Injuns even more than they hates me.'

NINE

There was a swiftness in the small female which had not flagged even after more than an hour of relentless running. Squirrel Sally had left the stagecoach and its six-horse team far behind her, knowing that she could make better progress through the tree-covered hillside on foot. With her trusty rifle clutched in her hands Squirrel Sally kept on running. Nothing could stop her in her quest to find Iron Eyes.

She had been following the trail of hoof-tracks left by the infamous rider's high-shouldered palomino stallion with the same mastery for which the bounty hunter was renowned. It was starting to get darker but she knew that there was still at least an hour of daylight left before the eventual coming of nightfall.

Plenty of time to catch up with the man she hunted.

The rolling wooded hills were covered in the sort

of wild undergrowth she was used to. The forest reminded her of the one just above the ranch where her family had been slain only weeks earlier. She had practically lived in those woods, hunting game for the pot until that fateful day.

Now, like Iron Eyes himself, Squirrel Sally was hunting a man and not mere game. Every broken twig and branch was observed by her keen instincts and, just like the bounty hunter she was trailing, Sally was not slowed down by the barbs and thorns that tore at her flesh.

With the agility of a wildcat Squirrel Sally kept on moving relentlessly in pursuit of the elusive Iron Eyes. Every sinew in her small form told her she was closing the distance between them. It was as though she could actually sense where he was ahead of her.

Her tiny bare feet were used to the rugged terrain beneath them as she headed towards the summit of yet another hilltop. No boot leather was as hardy as the soles of her feet.

As she ran Sally thought about the mysterious dirt-track road which was carved through the dense forest. Every now and then she had caught a glimpse of it through the maze of trees. It was close to where she was running.

Hacking down a barrier of jagged vines with the barrel of her Winchester, Sally wondered if Iron Eyes had even noticed the road as he had trailed the wanted outlaw into this untamed land.

She doubted it. She had not known the deadly

bounty hunter long but it had been long enough for her to know that Iron Eyes never faltered from his chosen prey. He would ride through a wall of flames without even noticing if the man he was hunting was ahead of him. Nothing ever distracted the lethal Iron Eyes.

Like him, Sally would not quit.

Not until her task was over.

Although she did not know it, her new clothes were ripped and torn by the ravages of the treacherous terrain. Her arms and legs bled from a score of cuts but she raced on regardless. Then, as she battled onwards she felt something beneath her feet.

At first she assumed it was a puddle of water, but then her hunting brain told her that water was never sticky. Squirrel Sally stopped and ran the back of her shirt sleeve across her sweating brow. Her beautiful eyes stared back at the imprints of her own feet in the soft ground.

Sally felt her heart skip a beat.

Water was clear. Mud was brown. The puddle she had stepped in was vivid crimson. She knew of only one thing apart from her new shirt that was red.

She moved back cautiously then stopped.

The pool of blood was still rippling where she had stepped into it. It shimmered in the rays of the sun far above her. A thousand fears raced through her.

Not fears for her own safety but fears for the man

she was desperately searching for.

Her mouth grew dry.

'Hell,' she muttered. Her eyes looked all around her in search of a body. There was none to be seen. She rubbed her chin and frowned. 'This might be the blood of the varmint Iron Eyes was hunting. Sure, that's it.'

She did not believe her own words.

Her heart was now aching inside her. She swung around and looked to where the hoof tracks led. About 200 yards away she could see huge boulders on the top of the hill, bathed in sunlight. Between the boulders and herself a thousand trees of various types stood proudly.

Then she saw the arrows.

So many arrows embedded in only a few of the trees.

Reluctantly Squirrel Sally made her way up the slope towards one of the trees. The one with the most arrows in its trunk. She paused when she reached it.

The droplets of blood which spattered the tree trunk between the arrows were telling her hunter's brain a story. She did not like the story.

'Ya dumb galoot,' she scolded the bounty hunter as her eyes surveyed the ground around her feet. 'Ya had to git yaself tangled up with a bunch of redskins, didn't ya? Any critter with half a mind knows it don't pay to tussle with Injuns. If they done killed ya it's ya own damn fault, Iron Eyes.'

Then she saw the boot marks in the mud.

Her man's boot marks.

Squirrel Sally knew that Iron Eyes had not died here. He had managed to run. He was hurt but still able to run. She felt renewed hope swelling up inside her. Like a seasoned hound on the trail of a racoon Sally followed the trail of boot marks as they wound between the trees. Every now and then she encountered more arrows stuck in the trunks of trees where Iron Eyes must have taken cover.

Slowly she realized where the bounty hunter had been heading as he had tried to get away from the Indians. She focused hard on the boulders which rested on the top of the hill. They, unlike the rest of the forest, were bathed in brilliant rays of the dying sun.

'There,' she said knowingly. 'Ya went there to fend them off, didn't ya?'

The youngster ran up the final fifty feet or so of the slope until she reached the first of the massive boulders. Then she stopped abruptly.

Her eyes narrowed and she felt her stomach churn.

The smooth side of the mighty rock was smeared in blood where she knew Iron Eyes must have rested. More of the scarlet gore covered the ground. A lot of blood.

Too much blood, she told herself.

She gripped the rifle firmly in her hands and looked all around the area. Where were the bodies?

The bodies of the Indians she felt Iron Eyes would have killed as he tried to fight off his attackers.

There were no bodies of Indians, or anyone else for that matter. There was only an awful lot of blood, and so many footprints she could not count them all.

'Where are ya, Iron Eyes?' Sally whispered to herself as she studied the ground more carefully. 'Is ya dead? If'n ya are then where the hell is ya damn carcass?'

She was feeling her heart breaking inside her and was about to scream out in frustrated rage when her keen hearing caught a sound to her right. The small female cranked the rifle's mechanism as she swung around to face the direction from where she could hear the noise coming.

Chains rattling told her that another wagon was making its way through the dense, forested hills along the road. Without even knowing why, Sally sprung into action and raced away from the scene of carnage towards the sound. She had run a good 200 yards when she reached a high ledge above the dirt track road.

Sally leaned against a tree trunk and stared down at the road. Within a few seconds the wagon appeared below her.

Silently she watched.

This wagon was headed into and not out of the woods.

Her keen eyes stared down.

Unlike the two other wagons she had spied earlier, this one was empty. Its canvas was rolled up neatly on its flatbed. She was about to return to the boulders when Sally saw three riders following the vehicle.

Her eyes widened.

'The mayor,' she said curiously to herself. 'What in tarnation is that fancy dude doing here?'

TEN

The stout broad-branched tree might have proved a daunting hindrance to most young men but to Squirrel Sally it was nothing but a way of her ascending to a height where she might be able to get a better view of the terrain which lay ahead of her. She knew exactly in what direction Iron Eyes had been taken by the blood which marked his trail, but how far the Indians had gone was another, unanswered, question.

She was about fifty feet off the ground when she saw the smoke twisting its way up into the darkening sky. The glow of a large fire seemed to paint the surrounding trees in a devilish light.

Every inch of her tiny frame told her that that was where they had taken Iron Eyes. Her Iron Eyes. That was the Indian camp. That was her destination. The place where she would find her man again. She glanced upward. Nightfall was close now and soon a million stars and a half-moon would replace the setting sun. The distant fire would lead her straight to the Indian camp as the sky grew ever darker.

Licking her lips the young female gripped on to a branch with one hand whilst her other gripped her rifle. She hung perilously as she studied the land between herself and the campfire. She knew it was no more than a mile away.

Sally swung around and started back down towards the forest floor. Then she heard the haunting sound of drumming as it travelled on a wisp of wind and found her ears.

'Injun drums,' Sally said as expertly she climbed down. 'I wonder if'n that's good or bad.'

As a million fears spread through her she continued down to the ground. What if she had to fight those Indians? What if they were as ornery as Iron Eyes himself? Could she get the better of a whole herd of them?

She dropped the last ten feet and landed surefooted beside the broken brush and the trail of blood. Then for the first time she spotted the hooftracks beside the footprints. They were the hoofmarks of the palomino stallion. Those Indians had taken not only Iron Eyes with them, but his horse as well.

Squirrel Sally straightened up and rested the Winchester on her right shoulder. The sound of drumming seemed fainter at ground level, she thought.

Fainter, but still audible.

She began to run towards the drumming.

With each step she thought about the man she had been hunting for what seemed so long and yet was in reality only a matter of days. Was it possible for him still to be alive? she asked herself as her pace increased.

Could anyone lose that much blood and still be alive?

And why had the Indians taken him with them?

Iron Eyes had to be alive.

Squirrel Sally was now running. Running faster than she had ever run before. With each step the smell of the distant fire grew stronger in her nostrils.

She was running with the speed only someone young could ever achieve.

'Ya better not be dead, Iron Eyes,' Sally panted. 'I'll surely kill ya if'n ya are.'

There was a sense of excitement throughout the small encampment of wigwams. The Indians were getting more and more feverish as the drumming increased in volume and both men and women alike danced around the clearing. The bells around their ankles played a haunting tune. The blood-red flames of the campfire were dancing as well. They licked the sky, sending sparks floating up toward the cloudless sky. There was going to be a sacrifice this day and it would be a human one.

106

Yet Iron Eyes still refused to scream out and acknowledge his pain as half a dozen sturdy men grabbed his hair and arms and hauled him to his feet. The bounty hunter had never endured anything quite so agonizing before. Blood had begun to trail again from his numerous wounds long before he had been dragged upright. With each drop of the scarlet gore he felt his strength fading to a place he knew only the dead could withstand.

For a few seconds they supported their thin gaunt prisoner as women threw dirt and stones into his gruesome face. A hundred insults were also tossed at the bounty hunter but words had never hurt him. Only bullets and arrows had ever managed to trouble the once vigorous man. Iron Eyes remained silent and brooding. A thousand plans darted through his still fertile imagination, but he had no strength left to execute any of them. He only remained upright because the Indians were holding him. He knew that if they released their grip he would fall flat on to the ground again like a rag doll.

One of the Indians was dressed in more elaborate clothing than the others. He wore a cloak made of the fur of a bear, and a horned buffalo skull over his painted face. Iron Eyes knew that this was their medicine man. He moved closer and berated their prisoner with words and handfuls of some strange dust, which he kept tossing at the blood-soaked bounty hunter.

Defiantly Iron Eyes stared through his mane of

limp hair at the medicine man and remained totally silent, even though he realized that this man was probably the one who was encouraging the others to kill him.

The braves had practically to carry Iron Eyes towards the wooden stake as his feet and legs no longer seemed able to obey his still sharp mind. He silently cursed them all for what they were doing to him, but he understood their actions.

He was an intruder in their land.

He was also Iron Eyes.

Contrary to his first impressions of these unfamiliar Indians they were exactly like all of their native brothers. They seemed to hate and want to kill him just like all of the other tribes he had known over the years. Iron Eyes dragged in air and then thought about all of the white men who also hated him. It seemed that just being who and what he was suited no one. Everyone with half a mind wanted to kill him.

Iron Eyes jerked his head up. His mane of long black hair whipped up and over his scarred face and landed on his broad shoulders.

He heard a few of the females gasp when they set eyes on the face which bore the scars of every one of his battles. His eyes, half-closed, darted from one face to another whilst the six braves used strips of wet rawhide to tie his arms firmly behind the stake. The bounty hunter knew that wet rawhide tended to tighten around flesh and cut through it when it dried out. Was this yet another torture they had planned for him? he asked himself. Not satisfied with him bleeding to death or being roasted like a hog they wanted to see his bones protruding out of his wrists when the leather sliced through his skin.

The sturdy Indians released their grip on their captive and stepped over the kindling, away from the pitiful creature they had captured.

Iron Eyes slumped forward. The leather strips held him in check as the bounty hunter watched the angry crowd start to bring arms full of even more dried kindling towards him.

They piled it up all around the already charred wooden stake. Then their high pitched wailing started once more. His eyes glanced to his side. He had been right, he thought. There were at least a dozen older men seated on the ground in a line. Each of them sporting a bonnet of eagle feathers. Each pounding his drum with some sort of stick.

Iron Eyes inhaled deeply and looked up at the slowly darkening sky above the clearing. A thought occurred to Iron Eyes. One which might have amused him if he were not racked by so much pain that he had begun to ignore it. You had to believe in some sort of god for there to be salvation from this kind of problem.

But there would be no divine intervention to save him unless the Devil himself was watching. His head felt like a heavy weight on his thin neck. It fell forward and his chin touched the blood-stained collar of his ragged shirt.

He was going to die.

Die damn slowly.

How long could a critter last when being burned at a stake? he asked himself. Maybe too long.

He had been burned before. Had had skin melting on his bones until he was begging to be allowed to die. That had been hundreds of miles away but the memory was like his scars.

It remained.

Then he saw two warriors appear from behind a wigwam. Their blazing torches spat out sparks of venom. They were dancing as they made their way through the crowd towarda their defenceless victim.

The bounty hunter sighed.

He shook his head.

The two warriors came closer to the helpless Iron Eyes, who was hanging from his tethers. His cold bullet-coloured eyes watched their every movement, yet he still said nothing.

Some men might have begged for mercy. Begged to be allowed to flee, but that was not his way. Iron Eyes did not beg anyone for mercy, for it was something he did not understand.

The singing erupted again at the sight of the torches. None but the bounty hunter remained tight-lipped. Drums pounded and the Indians with bells on their ankles started to encircle the man tied to the stake. Voices, drums and bells combined to fill the clearing with the most chilling of melodies.

It was the song of death.

Iron Eyes shook his head and glared at them through the limp strands of his hair as they moved as though one being. The torches were held aloft as the two braves started to chant their rituals at the sky above them whilst the medicine man again threw dust over their victim. Iron Eyes glanced at the kindling which was stacked well above his belt buckle.

He was doomed.

The song of death grew even louder.

ELEVEN

It seemed like a whole lifetime since he had encountered the Lucas gang back at San Angelo and had efficiently destroyed them all without even breaking a sweat. A lifetime since he had set out on the trail of Joe Kane and made the mistake of entering what he now knew to be Indian territory. What a difference a few hours could make to even the strongest of men. Now Iron Eyes was virtually helpless. Helpless and staring into the very jaws of death itself.

The bounty hunter lifted his head and gave out a long painful sigh. The dancing medicine man encouraged the two braves with the torches. They needed little spurring. They were thrusting the fiery torches at their defenceless captive. Taunting him like a cat with a mouse. The sparks flew in all directions over the tinder-dry kindling as the torches hit Iron Eyes in his face and blood-soaked body.

The flames of the torches might have hurt an

uninjured man but Iron Eyes was already racked with more pain than he had ever felt before. Mere torches only annoyed rather than added to his agony. It was like having hornets stinging you whilst a bear gnawed on your bones.

Iron Eyes focused past the blood which dripped from the strands of limp wet hair that hung before his eyes. He kept looking at the excited crowd. The last time he had seen such mass hysteria had been ten years ago at a public hanging back in El Paso. Now it was he who was on the gallows, but Iron Eyes knew it would be fire and not a rope that concluded his emaciated existence.

Once the torches were dropped to the pile of kindling that surrounded the stake against which he was secured Iron Eyes realized that he would be engulfed in flames.

Suddenly he noticed every one of the Indians turn and look to where the sound of approaching hoofs resounded. Then Iron Eyes saw them. Three riders astride thundering horses entered the camp. Within a couple of seconds the singing had stopped, as had the incessant drumming and the dancing.

Iron Eyes was surprised. His sore eyes looked to where the three Indian horsemen were bringing their painted ponies to an abrupt halt next to the largest of the wigwams. They threw themselves from their mounts and raced to the medicine man and the warriors holding the torches.

One of the men was screaming at the medicine man and his two cohorts. Not one word came in reply to the rantings which spewed at them from the muscular man.

Iron Eyes tilted his head and stared from the stake to which he was firmly bound. The loudest of the three horsemen drew his attention.

Even half-dead the bounty hunter seemed to recognize the shouting Indian. This one man had the ability to make them all cower in submission. Whoever he was, he had authority and knew how to use it.

Iron Eyes began to reason that the shouting brave must be their chief. His looks were also very familiar to the bounty hunter's sore eyes.

After what felt like an eternity to the Indians' prisoner the two warriors holding the blazing torches walked sheepishly away and deposited their the fiery sticks into the already fearsome campfire. As they did so the medicine man also shied away.

Iron Eyes tried to swallow but there was no spittle. All he could do was look at the face of the man who, for some unknown reason, had saved him. A face that his tired soul seemed to know.

'Who are ya?' Iron Eyes croaked.

There was no reply. The brave turned and looked up into the gruesome features of the bounty hunter hanging by his arms from the wooden stake. His expression was grim as he waved at the men on either side of him to untie Iron Eyes.

114

Both braves obeyed and cut the rawhide restraints, then they held the weak bounty hunter upright between them.

'It has been a long time since we last met, Iron Eyes,' the confident warrior said as the blood-drenched bounty hunter was helped across the dried kindling towards him. 'Many moons have come and gone since we last looked into each other's eyes.'

Iron Eyes raised an eyebrow and peered into the face of the Indian who had saved him from execution. He seemed to recognize the face but could not remember from where or when he might have come close to an Indian who did not try to kill him.

'Who are ya?' Iron Eyes asked feebly. 'How'd ya know me?'

'Do you not recall when your life was saved by a wolf, my old friend?' the brave asked. He turned and walked towards the largest of the wigwams. 'Bring him to my lodge.'

The sturdy silent braves assisted Iron Eyes to follow their chief. Step by step the long thin legs of the wounded bounty hunter managed to keep level with his helpers.

'A wolf?' the bounty hunter repeated, then he felt a cold shiver trace through his entire frame. Suddenly the face of the man became as it was when he had last encountered it. Then it had been the face of a youngster. A mere youth who had claimed that he could miraculously change into a wolf

115

simply by wishing to do so.

A wolf had then saved the life of the bounty hunter.

But that had been after Iron Eyes had thought the young Indian he knew as Silent Wolf had been killed. He was confused as he forced his legs to work.

'Silent Wolf?' Iron Eyes croaked.

The brave lifted a blanket up from the entrance of the wigwam and allowed his two men to help the injured bounty hunter to enter the large structure. He followed, and when Iron Eyes had been helped to sit down on a mattress of bearskins he stood opposite and stared at the man who had tasted the wrath of his tribe and barely survived. He muttered a few words to the two Indians and they left the lodge.

'I recall a critter who called himself Silent Wolf,' Iron Eyes said. 'I thought ya was dead.'

'You do remember, my old friend. Yes, I was known as Silent Wolf, but now I have another name. All chiefs have to change their name when they are chosen to lead their people.'

'This handful of people is all that's left of ya tribe?'

Silent Wolf nodded. 'Yes. We were once like the leaves on the trees but now we are few.'

Iron Eyes could not disguise his agony. He gritted his teeth and kept rubbing his wrists in an attempt to get what little blood he still had left in his veins to start flowing again.

'What they call ya now?' he asked.

There was no sign of any emotion on the face of the chief as he shrugged. 'It does not matter. To you I shall always be Silent Wolf. You may call me that.'

'I thought ya was dead,' Iron Eyes said again.

'In many ways I was.' The chief nodded. 'But like you I do not die easy.'

'Did ya really change into a wolf?' Iron Eyes had never been able to solve the puzzle that had dogged his memory for so many long, hard years. 'A wolf saved my bacon. I looked right into that critter's eyes and I always reckoned that I saw you looking right back at me. Was it you?'

'It was so very long ago.' Silent Wolf gestured with his hands. 'I cannot argue with your memory, old friend. If you say I changed into a wolf, then I did.'

Iron Eyes looked long and hard at the expressionless Indian. 'Ya either telling the truth or ya the best damn liar I ever met, Silent Wolf.' Iron Eyes poked a hand into one of his trail-coat pockets and pulled out a sodden blood-soaked cigar. He put it into the corner of his mouth and produced a match. His thumbnail scratched its tip. It erupted into flame. He sucked the flame into the black cigar.

'So ya the chief of this meagre bunch?'

Silent Wolf nodded. 'Yes.'

'Then how come ya braves bushwhacked and nearly killed me, Silent Wolf?' Iron Eyes sucked in

117

more smoke and savoured its flavour. 'Not a very neighbourly thing to do to an old pal.'

'I sent them just to bring you to me for I need your help,' Silent Wolf explained. 'I did not want you to be hurt. My words were not understood. They killed the man you were hunting and then realized that they had to bring you back here. My medicine man thought I wished you tortured and slain. I wanted you fit, not as you now are. Forgive me.'

'Hell. Don't go fretting none.' Iron Eyes nodded. 'Besides, I'm used to being shot up. My wounds hardly have time to heal before some bastard adds another one. How'd ya know I was in ya forest, anyways?' Iron Eyes blew a line of smoke at the ground.

The chief paced around the interior of his lodge. Then he paused and looked at the badly injured man. 'I have many eyes which tell me many things, Iron Eyes. I knew you were close but when you entered the forest I sent a hunting party to get you. To bring you to me.'

'Like I said, ain't no call fretting none, Silent Wolf,' Iron Eyes said. He ran bloody fingers through his mane of limp black hair. 'If ya was that wolf that saved my bacon I reckon I owes ya my life anyway. Did ya really change? Did ya?'

'Could a boy change into a wolf?' the chief asked wryly.

'I'm still trying to figure that one out, boy.'

An expressionless Silent Wolf remained by the opening of the wigwam as two females rushed in with bowls of hot water whilst another carried a pot of aromatic soup. The chief spoke in his native tongue to them. The females nodded and knelt beside the seated bounty hunter.

'What these womenfolk intending on doing?' Iron Eyes asked as the women peeled the sticky blood-drenched trail coat and shirt from his thin scarred body.

'They will wash and tend your wounds,' Silent Wolf answered. 'And feed you.'

'Just tell 'em my boots and pants stays right where they are, Silent Wolf,' Iron Eyes grunted. 'I've sure had my fill of frisky females trying to get my pants off me.'

The chief translated the instructions. The women giggled as others now entered their chief's domain.

Wearily Iron Eyes watched as his gore-sodden clothes were taken away by one of the women. 'What in tarnation did ya want me here for anyways, Silent Wolf? I'm betting it weren't for scrubbing my old trail gear. So why'd ya want me here?'

The chief folded his arms and looked down at the man with the horrific wounds. He stepped forward.

'I need you to help me, Iron Eyes. Only you can help me.'

Iron Eyes squinted up at his saviour. 'How exactly do ya figure I can help ya? Help ya with what?'

'My daughter has been taken by white men.

119

White men who violate our land,' Silent Wolf
answered. 'Their leader warned me that if my
people try again to free her they will kill her.'

'How old is she, Silent Wolf?' There was genuine
concern in the bounty hunter's voice as he stared
through the smoke of the twisted cigar in his
scarred lips.

'She is only nine summers old,' came the reply.

A surge of strength somehow filled the bruised
and battered Iron Eyes. He straightened up in defi-
ance of his horrific injuries. 'What ya want me to
do? Whatever it is, I'm game.'

'Before you were so badly wounded I wanted you
to find my daughter and bring her back to me.'
Silent Wolf turned away as though he were embarrassed. 'But now you are hurt. A strong Iron Eyes
could have done it easily but my foolish braves have
destroyed any chance of—'

'I ain't dead or even close to it,' Iron Eyes
growled. 'I can still find and rescue her, boy. Don't
ya go doubting that.'

Silent Wolf inhaled deeply. 'I have never known
another like you, old friend. Never met anyone as
brave.'

'I ain't brave,' the bounty hunter corrected. 'I'm
just plain ornery and I don't cotton to folks hurting
young 'uns.'

'I fear that they have already killed her,' the chief
said.

'Knowing you I'd have thought that ya would

120

have gone after her already, Silent Wolf,' the bounty hunter said bluntly.

'We did but we have no guns,' Silent Wolf responded. 'We did try and I lost half of my braves to the white men's rifles. It was then that their leader warned me that the next time he would slay my little girl.'

As his wounds were being washed clean Iron Eyes nodded. 'But ya know where them white men have their hideout? Right?'

'Yes. They have a ranch and a silver mine on either side of the forest,' Silent Wolf told him. 'My daughter might be in either place.'

Iron Eyes was handed a bowl of hot soup. He downed it and then shook his head as his body absorbed its goodness. 'Listen up. I got me a bottle of whiskey in my saddle-bags, Silent Wolf. Get that for me. I need me some fire in my belly.'

The words had only just left the lips of the bounty hunter when one of the braves with whom the chief had ridden into camp came in through the entrance of the wigwam, carrying the very same bottle Iron Eyes had described. The brave handed it to Silent Wolf, who in turn gave it to the dishevelled Iron Eyes. A slight smile etched the gruesome face as Iron Eyes raised the neck of the bottle to his teeth and yanked the cork free.

'Obliged, Silent Wolf,' the injured man said after spitting the cork across the wigwam. 'Now I'm gonna heal damn quick.'

The chieftain watched as the weary man gulped down most of the bottle's contents before lowering it.

The injuries were washed and sewn up as Iron Eyes poured the remainder of the fiery liquor over his chest and back. He tossed the bottle away. As the women scurried away he somehow forced himself back up on to his shaking legs. He staggered and went to stand beside the troubled Indian.

'Ya fretting,' Iron Eyes said. 'Ain't no call. I'll track down ya daughter and bring her back to ya.'

Silent Wolf looked at the half-dead creature he remembered from his youth and rested a hand on the bounty hunter's bony bare shoulder. 'I fret for you, my friend,' he said. 'My braves have hurt you badly. I have never seen anyone so close to death as you were when I returned to camp. It is a miracle that you are still alive. I do not think that you can take on so many white eyes and survive.'

Iron Eyes gave a grunt. He walked to the entrance of the wigwam and stared out. It was now almost dark above the camp.

'I don't die that easy, boy.' He glanced at the face of his friend and gave a nod. 'Besides, I'm not riding alone. I intend taking a few of ya braves with me. Even bows and arrows can do a lot of damage. I'm proof of that.'

Silent Wolf stepped next to Iron Eyes.

'I shall ride with you.'

Again the bounty hunter nodded. 'I figured ya

would say that, old friend. I guess having a man along with me that can change into a wolf might come in mighty useful. Unless ya lost the knack of doing that. Well? Have ya?'

'You shall see, Iron Eyes,' Silent Wolf replied.

'I'll be looking.' The bounty hunter stretched his aching frame and rubbed his lips with the palm of his left hand. 'Ya got any cigars around this camp?'

'We have only our peace pipes.'

Iron Eyes shook his head. 'Peace pipes? Nope. I reckon that ain't fitting when ya intending on starting a war.'

'Do you think we shall have to kill many men in order to free my child, Iron Eyes?'

The simple reply came fast and sharp. 'Yep. I'll kill 'em all if that's what it takes.'

Suddenly across the clearing the sound of disturbance filled the ears of everyone in the camp. Silent Wolf walked out of his wigwam with his ravaged friend Iron Eyes at his shoulder.

Both men stared beyond the wooden stake to where a cursing female was being carried by four warriors. The men somehow wavered as they brought Squirrel Sally into the light of the blazing torches.

'Who is it?' Silent Wolf asked.

Before Iron Eyes could answer, one of the Indian women came across the expanse of open ground from the river with the bounty hunter's shirt in her hands. What remained of its ancient fabric had been beaten on rocks until nearly all of the blood had been washed away. She walked up to Iron Eyes and showed it to him.

Iron Eyes gave a grateful nod of his head but all he could truly see was the irate Squirrel Sally as she fought with the men who had captured her.

'Do you know her?' Silent Wolf asked once more.

Again the brutally injured figure nodded. 'Yep.'

Then somehow the small female managed to wriggle, bite and kick her way free of the men who were carrying her. She swung around the neck of one of them and brought her foot violently up into his groin. He yelped and buckled.

Without a second's hesitation Sally jerked her knee up and caught the warrior's jaw. He fell like an axed tree. With the entire camp looking at the fallen brave his three companions leapt at the agile sprite.

Again Sally was more than a match for them. As one man reached down she ran up his back and kicked another in the face. His eyes rolled before he too fell. The long plaited hair of one of the braves was seized as Sally swung around and hit the other startled warrior in the chest with her small bare feet. When her feet landed on the ground she twisted and kicked both men as hard as she could in their necks, sending them cartwheeling over the already stricken men. Then faster than the blink of an eye her hands found her rifle again and she gave out a triumphant hoot.

Terrified, the Indian woman took cover with the wet shirt behind the half-naked bounty hunter.

Squirrel Sally held herself in a crouched position, with glaring eyes burning across the distance between herself and the chief's wigwam.

'Is ya OK, Iron Eyes darling?' she bellowed out. 'Reckon I saved ya life again. Was they about to scalp ya?'

The bounty hunter raised a bony hand. 'Easy with that toothpick, Squirrel. Don't go killing nobody.'

Sally took a step towards them and then noticed the Indian female hiding behind her bare-chested beloved.

'I see ya,' she snarled. 'What ya doing, taking my Iron Eyes's clothes off him? He's mine.'

Then her attention focused on the silent face of Iron Eyes.

'What in tarnation is ya up to, ya ugly varmint? Sowing some wild oats? Is that it?'

The chief looked up into the taller man's face.

'You know her?' Silent Wolf asked. 'Is she your woman, old friend?'

'I ain't got me no woman, Silent Wolf,' Iron Eyes said from the corner of his mouth. He kept watching as Sally came closer and closer to them. 'Trouble is, she kinda likes me.'

Sally was looking more and more angry the nearer she came to them. She pushed the hand-guard down and then back up in one quick movement. The Winchester was primed and ready for action.

The surrounding Indians ran for cover.

'I'm ready for some killing,' Squirrel Sally bellowed. 'I reckon I ought to shoot that little gal
behind ya first. She looks like she's the sort to steal
another gal's man.'

Again the bounty hunter waved his hand at her.

'Don't go doing nothing loco, Squirrel.'

'Loco?' Sally's face went crimson as rage fired up
inside her petite form. 'Did ya call me loco?'

'Ya don't understand,' Iron Eyes added. 'I ain't in
no danger and the little lady behind me only
washed the blood off my shirt.'

Sally kept advancing with the rifle levelled at
them.

The chief looked at his tall friend. 'Would she
shoot?'

'Yep. She will unless I can sweet-talk her.' Iron
Eyes sighed and stepped away from the Indians.
'The chief here is an old friend, Squirrel girl. He
needs my help.'

Sally snarled, then blasted a shot up into the
heavens and began to march towards both men.
'Eyewash. I reckon I found ya just before ya was
gonna do some lovemaking to these Injun gals, Iron
Eyes. How could ya cheat on me after us getting
betrothed an' all?'

Iron Eyes managed to raise a scarred eyebrow.
'Lovemaking?'

'Look at ya.' Squirrel was starting to choke on her

126

own tears as she closed the distance between them. 'Half-naked and all shiny like a new dime. No wonder these females can't keep their hands off ya. You're even prettier without ya clothes on than when ya fully dressed.'

'Ya wrong, Squirrel,' Iron Eyes urged. 'Calm down and think about this a while. My friend Silent Wolf wants me to go find and rescue his little daughter.'

'Butt naked?' Squirrel Sally yelped. 'I ain't gonna swallow that. Git out of the way, ya long thin galoot. I'm gonna blow her head off.'

'Put that rifle down, sweetheart,' Iron Eyes said firmly.

'And how come ya got a sowed-up hole in ya?' Sally raised the barrel and fired into the air again before cranking the spent casing out of the rifle's magazine.

'It's a long story.'

'Sounds like a damn tall one to me,' Squirrel Sally riposted.

'Put that rifle down,' Iron Eyes shouted.

As always she totally ignored him and advanced with the smoking barrel of the carbine aimed straight at his midriff. 'Did ya tell her that you're betrothed? Did ya?'

'Nope.' Iron Eyes shook his head.

Silent Wolf looked impressed by the unafraid female. 'So this is your woman, Iron Eyes? I like her. She has spirit.'

'My what?' the bounty hunter gasped. 'She ain't my woman.'

'Yes I is.' Sally stopped as her rifle barrel found the bounty hunter's belt buckle. She looked at each man in turn as she also tried to see the terrified female hiding behind them. 'Tell the truth, Iron Eyes darling. We're almost hitched.'

Iron Eyes snatched the rifle barrel and tore the weapon from her grasp.

'If I was gonna get hitched it sure wouldn't be to a loco gal who once shot me,' he announced.

Squirrel Sally watched as the bounty hunter turned and walked unsteadily back into the wigwam, carrying her smoking Winchester in his hands.

'Your name is Squirrel?' Silent Wolf asked as the Indian woman fled in terror.

She nodded. 'Yep. Iron Eyes is kinda shy about us being love birds.'

'Tell me. Did you really shoot him?' The chief gestured for her to follow the bounty hunter into his lodge. She did so.

Seated upon the rifle, Iron Eyes was drinking more of the soup and watching them with glaring annoyance.

'She ain't my woman,' he insisted. 'First time I met her she shot a chunk of my back off.'

She started to laugh. 'It sure was funny.'

Unlike the female, Silent Wolf did not smile. He looked down at the bounty hunter, who in turn was looking straight back at him. There was a knowing understanding between them which did not require words any longer.

Both knew that there was work to do this night.

Deadly work.

TWELVE

The night progressed in its usual fashion. A million creatures roamed through the darkness of the forested hills in search of prey as they had done since time began. To them this was just another period of darkness identical to all those which had preceded it, yet this night would prove to be very different from all those beneath the canopies of tree branches. This night there would be another kind of killing which had nothing to do with animals in search of food.

There was a fortune to be made shipping cheap Mexican silver across the border and Ben Calter had made his fortune several times over. But all of that was about to change.

What had run like a well-oiled wagon wheel for years had now suddenly taken another course. It was a course that the mayor of San Angelo did not like. Yet as it grew close to midnight nothing had actually happened to justify Calter's trepidation.

But Calter felt something was about to occur. Something which might destroy everything he had built up over the years. It all hinged on fear and that fear had been fuelled by the utterance of one name.

Iron Eyes.

Just knowing that the infamous Iron Eyes was in the vicinity had made him panic. For he, like all the other men wanted dead or alive in the West, knew that if the bounty hunter caught an outlaw's scent he never stopped chasing until one of them was dead. Calter had surrounded himself with twenty of the best hired guns money could buy over the years. They ferried his illegal cargo from Mexico through the dense forest into Texas. These men were like himself, wanted dead or alive. Each had a price on his head.

The trouble was that Ben Calter knew that even twice that many guns might not be able to stop the infamous bounty hunter from reaching him. He, like everyone else who knew the name of Iron Eyes, had heard the tall tales of how the skeletal man was more akin to a ghost than an actual living man. Calter knew that it was impossible to kill something that was already dead.

And Iron Eyes was close. Calter could sense it in every drop of his sweat. Perhaps the manhunter was here to find the outlaw once known as Rafe Bond. To find and kill him as he had mercilessly killed all the other lawbreakers he had ever encountered.

Calter realized that none of his hired gunfighters

would remain standing if Iron Eyes got them in his gun sights. The horrific creature must have made a pact with the Devil himself, Calter concluded. What other explanation could there be?

The night was cold across the border where the silver mines lay on the fringes of the trees. Hundreds of low-paid Mexicans slaved away in fear of their paymaster's wrath. It was cold but Calter was sweating, as all men sweat when they sense that their own existence is threatened.

There were three mines driven into the foundations of the great forested hillside. The Mexican miners worked day and night digging the precious ore out of each of them. On the tree-covered hillside above all three of the mine entrances air shafts had been drilled down to give the miners fresh air and allow any lethal gases to escape safely. The shafts were up to fifty feet deep.

A mere dozen yards from the mine entrances three large wooden huts had been built to accommodate the miners. Wagons and their teams of horses rested downwind of the huts next to a small locked log cabin. Within the cabin something even more precious than silver ore was kept. Calter had kept the small Indian girl prisoner to ensure that Silent Wolf and his braves did not attack again.

For months it had worked and the Indians had not attacked. But the little girl, who was a mere poker chip to Calter, had now become a lure. A lure which Iron Eyes would be drawn to in order to rescue her.

Calter's gamble was to backfire. She was the only reason the bounty hunter had not already ridden away from the forested hills.

Ben Calter paced anxiously up and down beneath the cabin's porch overhang.

Lum Barker was nearly as dangerous as he looked. He had killed more men in his time than he could accurately recall but he was loyal to Calter. He was the only one of the notorious outlaws who never questioned anything his boss came up with. Yet as Barker sat on the driver's board of one of their numerous wagons even he began to wonder why Calter seemed so skittish.

'What's wrong, Ben?' Barker asked as he chewed tobacco. He looked down at his boss. 'Ya looks like ya seen yaself a ghost.'

Calter paused and cast his attention up to the well-whiskered face above him. Until now he had not spoken to any of his men about his concerns. He realized that even well paid as they all were, none of them would want to face the legendary bounty hunter.

'What ya mean, Lum?' Calter tried vainly to appear as though there was nothing wrong. Barker was far too wise to fall for that.

'I mean that ya bin all knotted up since ya come back from town earlier,' Barker observed. He spat a lump of brown goo into the moonlight. 'Nervous as a cat on a hot tin roof.'

'I ain't.'

Barker chuckled. 'Something's eating at ya craw, Ben. The rest of the boys ain't smart enough to notice but I is. I knows when a critter is troubled. What is it?'

Calter ran a hand across the back of his wet neck. 'I learned something earlier and it ain't something that makes a man hanker to be like you and me, Lum. Wanted men.'

Barker paused his chewing and leaned over towards his boss.

'What ya learned that's gotten ya so fretful, Ben?'

Again Calter wondered if he dared tell even Barker the truth about why he was so worried. Could he trust his top gun not to hightail it when the name of Iron Eyes was uttered? If he ran then they all would.

'There's a bounty hunter in the area, Lum,' Calter said.

Barker gave a nod and spat. 'Ain't the first time.'

'A bounty hunter we've all heard tell of,' Calter added, nervously watching Barker's reaction. 'I was feared he might find our road through the forest and head on here to try his luck.'

'We've handled bounty hunters before, Ben,' Barker said, resuming his chewing. 'But I never done seen ya get all troubled like ya are before. This critter must be mighty good at his job.'

Ben Calter rested a hand on the wagon's brake pole and gazed down at the shadows. 'I hear that he's more than good at his job, Lum. I heard tell he never fails to collect bounty on anyone he decides to hunt.'

Lum Barker nodded knowingly. 'Ya don't mean. . . ?'

Calter nodded even harder than his top gun. 'Ya know who I mean, Lum?'

'Iron Eyes?' Barker whispered the name as though he was afraid that if any of Calter's other men heard it they would immediately ride.

'Yep.' Calter returned his eyes to Barker's bearded face. 'He was in San Angelo last night. Rode out, but the boys at the ranch say he never passed there. That means he must be in the forest someplace.'

Barker slowly climbed down from the wagon. His face was grim even in the eerie illumination of a half-moon. He removed his Stetson briefly to wipe his brow on his jacket sleeve.

'Iron Eyes ain't one to tangle with.'

'I know,' Calter agreed. 'He killed the entire Lucas gang last night and then went after Joe Kane.'

'Then Joe is a dead man,' Barker said.

'But where is he now?' Calter bit his lip.

Lum Barker looked around at the half-dozen other gunmen in the area as they rifle-whipped the miners heading into the mines. He knew the major-ity of the other gunmen were miles away at the ranch.

'Don't go telling anyone else about Iron Eyes,'

Barker said. He spat the spent tobacco plug away. 'None of these boys got the vinegar to face him. They'll run if they even hear his name, Ben.'

Calter turned and looked at the cabin behind them. 'What we gonna do with the Indian girl? I was thinking it might be better to take her to the ranch.'

Barker pushed his coat tails over his gun grips and rested his knuckles on them. 'We should never have taken that gal from them Injuns, Ben. I told ya that at the time. She's trouble.'

'It stopped them Injuns attacking us.'

'She might bring that critter down on us, Ben.'

'But why?'

'Iron Eyes ain't just a killer,' Barker said. 'I heard tell he likes to act the hero sometimes. If he's heard about her being held prisoner here he might come looking.'

Calter shook his head and stared fearfully at the black screen of trees that faced them over the mine entrances. 'Where the hell is Iron Eyes?'

Lum Barker pulled a block of tobacco from his pocket and bit off a large chunk. He started to chew slowly as he too watched the forest.

'If he's in there I figure we'll find out damn soon.'

'We gotta warn the boys.'

Lum Barker stepped towards the mines. 'Yep. But no mention of Iron Eyes.'

Calter sighed heavily.

THIRTEEN

The smell of the Indians' campfire hung on the still damp shirt and trail coat which draped the bounty hunter, yet he did not notice anything except the constant pain which continued to tear through his every sinew. Resembling a phantom more than a living man Iron Eyes sat astride his powerful palomino, staring ahead through the twilight as the sturdy animal obeyed its master's spurs and moved cautiously ahead.

The forest seemed to become more dense the further the bounty hunter ventured. The vegetation was becoming less brutal the higher they rode up the last of the rolling, tree-covered hills. Every part of the hunter's being told him that soon he would have his prey in sight. Soon he would have the chance to try to keep his promise to Silent Wolf.

A massive boulder similar to the ones among which Iron Eyes had taken refuge earlier faced his burning eyes beyond the array of trees. The light of

the half-moon seemed to make the smooth rock
sparkle as though it were covered in precious jewels,
but there were no jewels here. Only the biting frost
which also rimed the tops of the leafy canopies high
above him. The ground was as though a carpet of
thin ice had been sprinkled across its surface. It
crackled beneath the hoofs of the stallion.

This was no adventure for a man starved of so
much of his once abundant supply of blood to
undertake, but Iron Eyes had vowed to help his old
friend. Vowed to find and rescue Silent Wolf's
young daughter from the hands of the men who
were using her as a pawn in a very deadly game of
chess. Only death could stop the weary bounty
hunter from keeping his promise. Anything less
would either be endured or ignored.

Iron Eyes swayed on his ornate Mexican saddle
but the firm thighs of Squirrel Sally prevented him
from falling from his high perch. Her strong young
arms also supported his skeletal frame whilst her
hands held on to his reins and steered the large
horse ever onward. With each purposeful stride of
the stallion Iron Eyes stared ahead at the gigantic
rock that they were approaching.

'I hear me something, Iron Eyes,' Sally said as she
nestled into his bony back. 'Do ya hear it?'

'Yep.' The long mane of black hair moved as Iron
Eyes gave a jerk of his head. He turned in a vain
attempt to see his fearless companion. 'I hear me
men toiling. Hammers and the like hitting rock. We

must be getting close to that silver mine.'

'Yeah, that's what I hears. Gotta be miners.' Sally squeezed him as she looked around the area with searching eyes. 'Where the hell did the chief go? He was right behind us on that pinto pony a few minutes back. Now he's up and vanished.'

Iron Eyes smiled. 'Reckon old Silent Wolf has himself a plan all of his own, Squirrel. I'm just bullet fodder he intends using to get the drop on them varmints.'

'What ya mean?'

'He knows I can draw their fire.'

'I surely don't like the sound of that.'

The stallion kept walking ever upward towards the boulder which loomed three times taller than the horse itself. Sally leaned and looked around his left shoulder at the face of the pale bounty hunter.

'How come ya knows him anyways?' she asked. 'I thought ya hated Injuns. Seems kinda odd to me that ya knows each other and one of ya ain't dead.'

'It's a long story,' Iron Eyes answered with a sigh.

'But he was meant to help us and not up and go wandering all on his lonesome,' Sally nagged. 'I reckon he's changed his mind and thought better of tangling with them gun-toting varmints.'

'Ya wrong. Silent Wolf is the only thing in this damn forest we can trust, Squirrel,' Iron Eyes replied. 'He'll not let us down. He got himself a way of bettering bad folks but he needs my shooting-irons to give him the chance of doing it.'

'I don't understand,' she admitted.

'Reckon I don't either.'

The sound of activity grew louder as the stallion reached the boulder. Squirrel Sally drew rein, dragged her rifle from under the saddle and dropped to the ground. She reached up and helped the unsteady bounty hunter to dismount before tying the reins around a tree stump.

She sniffed the air.

'I smell stove smoke.'

Iron Eyes leaned against his saddle. 'Yeah. Reckon they must be cold.'

'I'm too excited to be cold,' she said. 'What about you?'

He raised an eyebrow. 'I ain't got enough blood left in me to feel anything, Squirrel.'

Suddenly she became concerned. She looked at the tortured face of the man she somehow desired and saw his bleached features clearly for the first time. It was as though every drop of blood had been drained from his scarred face. Now he truly resembled a ghost.

'Damn it all, Iron Eyes. Ya looks plumb awful.'

'Good,' the bounty hunter said. 'Then that means I looks the same way that I feel. I'd hate to feel this bad and look OK.'

Her small left hand gripped his bony wrist. His bullet-coloured eyes looked down at her.

'What we doing?' she asked. 'Ya half dead. How can ya take on a bunch of gunslingers when ya can't even stand up straight?'

Iron Eyes looked at the pair of Navy Colts jutting out from his pants belt. 'They'll do my bidding, gal. Even halfway to Hell I'm more than a match for any damn outlaw.'

'Ya figure they're wanted?'

'Gotta be.'

'But the mayor of San Angelo is one of them,' she pointed out. 'He might even be their boss. How can he be an outlaw?'

Iron Eyes forced himself away from his mount and staggered round the large boulder until he had a perfect view of the clearing below their high view-point.

'Hell. A mayor? Most of his breed are worse outlaws than the scum I usually trail, Squirrel. Down here on the edge of the border I reckon nearly all of the menfolk must be wanted someplace. No honest critter would be here willingly.'

Sally watched as the tall man rested his fragile frame against the smooth surface of the rock and pulled his guns in turn to check that they were loaded. She stepped to his side and suddenly saw the buildings below, and the men moving through the moonlight to and from the mine entrances. There were far more men than she had imagined.

'Holy cow. There's a herd of them. Are ya think-ing of killing all of them ornery critters down there, Iron Eyes?' she wondered. 'Coz I thought ya only killed men that was wanted. Men with prices on

141

their heads.'

'They're involved in kidnapping,' Iron Eyes drawled. 'That's signed their death warrant in my book.'

Squirrel Sally moved closer to the edge of the steep drop.

'Don't let 'em see ya, Squirrel.' The bounty hunter pulled her away from the edge of the slope. 'We gotta be sly about this so we have an advantage. If'n they spots either of us up here they'll come shooting thick and fast. I ain't feeling good enough to run around looking for cover.'

She leaned into him. 'I sure do love ya.'

'No ya don't,' Iron Eyes said firmly. 'Ya just got an itch, like all females. I ain't for scratching no itch.'

'When we getting hitched?' she cooed.

'Never.'

Sally pouted. 'Hang on a tad. Ya didn't answer me when I asked ya about them gunmen down yonder. Are we gonna kill them even if they ain't wanted?'

'Yep.'

'But ain't that breaking the law?'

'I reckon we're in Mexico and everyone knows there ain't no law to break south of the border, Squirrel gal.' Iron Eyes pulled her small hand from his pants pocket and moved to where he had a clear view of what was happening down in the clearing. 'Besides, there's only one real law when folks steals young 'uns.'

She looked at him with adoring eyes, which he

142

ignored. 'I ain't got a damn clue what ya gabbing on about, ya long streak of bacon. What kinda law ya talking about?'

Iron Eyes pulled the hammers back on both his Navy Colts and nodded knowingly to himself as he toyed with his deadly weapons.

'Gun law, Squirrel,' he said in a low whisper. 'Gun law.'

Far below the two onlookers Calter's henchmen were becoming more and more curious as to why Lum Barker had instructed them to be alert, vigilant and ready for gunplay. Barker had not spilled the beans as to who might be dropping in with his hoglegs blazing, but slowly the name of the infamous bounty hunter travelled around the clearing to each and every one of Calter's gunslingers. For they all knew that they had encountered several bounty hunters over the years and had never had a problem dispatching them. If Calter and Barker were troubled then it had to be serious. Real serious.

Only the deadly Iron Eyes could turn hardened outlaws into fretting creatures afraid of their own shadows.

Two of Calter's men strode across the clearing towards the small cabin with their hands resting on their gun grips. They squared up to both Calter and Barker as they stood beside the flatbed wagon, with more than a hint of alarm in their moonlit features.

'It's Iron Eyes, ain't it?' one of the outlaws named Tey Gibbons asked.

'It's gotta be him,' his companion added.

Barker glanced at his paymaster without uttering a word. He watched as Calter exhaled and nervously chewed the inside of his mouth.

'Does it matter?' Calter asked. 'I pay ya all a handsome wage to kill any critter that gives us grief, don't I? What's so troubling about Iron Eyes?'

Gibbons stepped closer. 'Ya knows the difference, Ben. We ain't talking about no normal varmint when we talks about him. That bastard ain't like no other manhunter. He's never bin bettered and ya knows it. If he's around here then any smart outlaw rides away fast.'

Calter sighed. 'But there gotta be a dozen of you boys in camp right now. Twelve men against one is mighty fine odds and no mistake. Even if he was to stumble on this mining camp he'd not stand a chance against all of you boys.'

'We're talking about Iron Eyes, Ben,' Gibbons growled. 'Ya knows his reputation. He never gets bettered. No amount of guns can stop that killer.'

'They reckons he's a ghost,' the other outlaw piped up.

Gibbons nodded. 'Yeah. And no living man can kill no ghost, Ben. I'm not hanging around here to end up another notch on his gun grip.'

'Me neither.'

'A couple of yella-bellies.' Barker spat goo at

144

them. 'Takes ya money when there ain't nothing to do but ride shotgun guard on a damn wagon, but when it comes to earning ya wages ya want to high-tail it out of here. Yella.'

Ben Calter looked at the two terrified men trembling before him and understood their reasoning. Yet unlike them he was not willing to simply run away from what might happen. He had to remain brave or lose everything he had built up over the years.

'I'll give a thousand bucks to the man that kills Iron Eyes if he shows up, Tey,' Calter said. 'A thousand bucks is a fortune and all it takes is one bullet to earn it.'

'A thousand bucks?' both outlaws echoed at the same moment.

'Yep. Just think of the women and liquor ya can buy with that kinda loot, boys.'

'Ya wasting ya time talking to this pair of yella dogs, Ben boy.' Barker spat more goo at the ground. 'They're for running away from the mere name of Iron Eyes. I told ya they was nothing but cowards when ya hired 'em.'

'Hard cash?' Gibbons queried. 'A thousand in hard cash?'

Calter nodded. 'Yep.'

Suddenly the two men looked more relaxed. They mumbled to each other, then grinned widely at their boss.

'Don't go telling the other boys about the

thousand bucks, Ben. We don't want to share that kinda money with any of them.'

As Calter and Barker watched the two outlaws returning to their posts a chilling sound swept over the entire site. As though fear had a way of finding a direct path to their gun hands, every one of the men in the clearing drew his gun and cocked the hammer.

Again the spine-tingling noise rang out from the blackness of the surrounding trees.

It was the howling of a wolf.

Iron Eyes had only just pulled his coiled rope free from the saddle horn of the high-shouldered stallion when the howling filled his and Sally's ears. A hint of a wry smile found his scarred face as he uncoiled the rope beside the boulder.

'A wolf,' Sally gulped, her eyes flashing in the light of the half-moon. 'Did ya hear it? A wolf.'

Iron Eyes did not reply as he carefully uncoiled the rope and studied the tree branches that hung over the very edge of the steep drop in front of them. He looked down at the three wooden huts far below. A score of other high trees loomed just beyond the small cabin; their topmost branches almost reached a height level with where he was standing.

Sally moved to his side and looked up into his face. 'Ya ain't gone deaf on me, has ya?'

'Nope,' the bounty hunter replied, looking at the

trees all around them. 'I heard it.'

'Is ya scared? I sure don't cotton to getting my backside chewed on by no damn wolf.' Sally held her rifle even more firmly in her tiny hands. 'How come ya ain't feared? Wolves can be mighty dangerous.'

Iron Eyes rested for a moment as he made a loop in the end of his rope and held it against his long thin right leg. 'How'd ya know it's a wolf?'

Her eyes darted all around the dark undergrowth which surrounded them. 'That ain't no coyote, Iron Eyes. It's a cotton-picking wolf.'

'Sure sounds like one, Squirrel.' Iron Eyes began to swing the rope loop at hip level. 'But it don't mean it is one.'

Sally looked confused, then she glanced at the stallion as it chewed on grass and another howl filled the wooded hillside.

'How come ya horse ain't spooking?' she asked. 'I never done seen no horse that ain't spooked when a damn wolf bellows out, Iron Eyes. How come he ain't spooking?'

'Maybe if'n he thought it was a real wolf he would.' The bounty hunter had built up momentum with his swinging rope. It had started to buzz like a nest of hornets as he released his grip and guided the lasso towards a distant tree branch, about a hundred feet from where they were standing.

His cold eyes narrowed as they saw the loop close

147

and tighten around a stout branch. Iron Eyes pulled back on the rope like a man reeling in a fish on a line.

'What ya mean by him being scared of a real wolf?' Sally asked as the bounty hunter tied the end of his rope around the trunk of a tree close to the giant boulder. 'That sure sounds like a real wolf to me.'

'Then maybe it is.'

Squirrel Sally screwed up her eyes as her bottom lip came jutting out towards her companion. 'Is ya gonna start talking sense, Iron Eyes? Is that a real wolf or ain't it?'

'Ask yaself,' the gaunt man posed. 'Where's Silent Wolf?'

'Ya mean it's him making that racket?'

'Maybe.' Iron Eyes dropped a gun in both of his trail-coat pockets, unbuckled his belt and slid it from its loops around his bony frame. 'Maybe not. The horse sure ain't scared like ya would think it would be.'

'Come to think about it, I heard tell of Injuns being able to make all kinda critter noises.' Sally nodded to herself. 'Is that it? Is the chief making the wolf sound to kinda scare them outlaws?'

Iron Eyes stared at his rope, then pulled on it a few times. It was strung between two trees and spanned the distance across the clearing to just beyond the cabin. It went directly over the small cabin below them. It was taut and more than

148

capable of taking his weight, he silently told himself.

'I always reckoned that my old pal had the ability to turn himself into a wolf, Squirrel,' Iron Eyes told her.

'What? I don't know what in tarnation ya talking about, but ya sounding loco to me.' Sally tried to touch his brow. 'Has ya got a fever? Is that it? Ya done gone crazy on me and thinks ya pal can turn himself into a damn wolf. Great. We're gonna try and save a little Injun gal from them varmints down there and ya starts talking like a gibbering idiot.'

Sally had not noticed that as she had been ranting on at him, Iron Eyes had looped his belt over the rope and wrapped each end of the weathered leather around his bony hands.

'When ya ready I'll be down there killing me some bad folks, Squirrel,' Iron Eyes told her. Then he ran off the edge of the wooden hillside and flew into the sombre illumination of a million stars and a half-hearted moon.

The howling increased all around the camp. Gibbons and his cronies were lured towards the tree-covered hills above the mine entrances whilst Calter and Barker were also drawn away from the cabin which held their prisoner. The nightmarish light danced along the barrels of the guns held in outstretched arms. Trembling fingers stroked well-used triggers as squinting eyes searched for a target to shoot at. The howling continued and none of the outlaws saw or heard anything else as the emaciated

149

figure hurtled along the rope above them.

The thin bounty hunter was travelling faster than he had considered possible towards the trees. Within a heartbeat he seemed to be travelling over the cabin. Without even considering the danger he let go of both ends of the belt and felt himself falling precariously down.

Luck was on the side of the brave.

Iron Eyes hit the shingles of the cabin roof with both boots. Somehow he managed to remain upright. His spurs rang out their haunting melody. Alerted to the unfamiliar sound behind them both Calter and Barker swung on their heels and saw the ominous figure standing high above them on the wooden roof, bathed in chimney smoke.

Calter screamed out as Barker fanned the hammer of one of his guns. Red-hot tapers of fiery lead cut through the crisp night air in search of the bounty hunter, but Iron Eyes was gone.

'Where'd he go, Ben?' Barker yelled out. He rammed his smoking Colt into a holster and dragged its twin from its resting place. 'Did ya see where the critter went?'

Calter did not answer. He was running like a terrified jack rabbit from a settler's rifle. As Tey Gibbons and the rest of the men raced to where Barker was still shooting Ben Calter reached the place where all of their numerous horses were corralled. He bent double and forced himself between the white poles, then he stood and tried to see which of the many horses milling around was his own mount.

Barker stopped firing as the rest of the dozen men reached his side. He reloaded both his guns and looked all around the area for any sign of the strange figure of whom he had only caught a glimpse seconds earlier.

'Was it him, Lum?' Gibbons asked as the men fanned out around the cabin. 'Was it Iron Eyes ya was shooting at?'

There was no time to answer for just as Barker pushed the last bullet into the smoking chamber of his .45 an eerie sight came into view just beyond the side of the small cabin.

It was Iron Eyes, holding both his Navy Colts in his bony hands. As billowing chimney smoke curled around the tall ghostlike creature the bounty hunter squeezed his triggers simultaneously. Plumes of gunsmoke spewed from both barrels as bullets tore into Barker.

Lum Barker felt the bullet which went through his heart; he staggered before falling. Tey Gibbons was about to speak when he felt his own body suddenly racked with pain. The outlaw's eyes looked down as blood started to spread across the front of his shirt.

'I bin hit,' Gibbons yelled out.

Iron Eyes fired again.

This time Gibbons felt the impact and toppled to the ground. He fired up into the heavens as another spine-freezing howl filled the clearing.

The rest of the outlaws blasted their guns in the direction from where they had seen the fatal shots come, but the elusive bounty hunter was nowhere to be seen.

Five of the men turned and ran for the corral, whilst the remaining outlaws defied their own terror and advanced.

It was the wrong thing to do.

For in the blink of an eye the bounty hunter was before them with his guns held at hip height. Just as the outlaws opened fire he threw himself forward, landed on his belly and fired with guns held in outstretched arms. The darkness was filled with the hot rods of deadly lead. He blasted his guns over and over again until the area was filled with blinding gunsmoke and the outlaws were laid out neatly in a line beside the bodies of Barker and Gibbons. Slowly, Iron Eyes rose to his feet.

Calter was panicking. He had managed to pick out his horse but the rest of the gun-shy animals in the corral were racing around, making it impossible for him to reach it.

'That's gotta be Iron Eyes,' one of the outlaws yelled to his comrades as they leapt over the fence poles and entered the corral beside their boss.

Ben Calter turned and stared through the bluish moonlight at the cabin as scores of miners came racing from the mines and fled into the forest.

Calter grabbed one of his hired men. 'Where's Lum?'

'Halfway to hell by my reckoning, Ben,' the man replied. Then he tore his way free of his paymaster and grabbed hold of the nearest saddled mount.

Before the mayor of San Angelo could utter another sound the outlaws forced their horses through the fence poles and spurred hard. As the riders neared the road the sound of a Winchester rang out its fearful tune. Time and time again rifle shots rained from the carbine's barrel.

Calter gulped hard and watched as every one of the riders were shot off their saddles.

'There's more than just Iron Eyes in this mess,' he said to himself. He managed at last to grab hold of his horse's reins and bring it close to him. 'Iron Eyes ain't alone after all. He got himself. . . .'

Suddenly he remembered the female. The girl who had been in search of the bounty hunter. She must be with him, he told himself as he stepped into his stirrup and mounted his horse.

Then he heard a ferocious growling just beyond the fence poles behind him. Calter dragged his leathers to his left and swung the horse around. His eyes widened as he saw it.

A wolf.

A wolf with blazing yellow eyes stood before him, defying him to move. It snarled as white foam dripped from its fangs. The horse reared up, sending Calter tumbling to the ground. The growling grew louder as the wolf moved closer

Scrambling desperately up on to his knees Ben

Calter looked all around him for his spilled gun. He saw it, grabbed it and cocked its hammer.

No sooner had he aimed the gun than the wolf sprang.

FINALE

Seeing the wolf launch itself at him, Ben Calter repeatedly fired his gun. The fearsome wolf hit him hard and started to tear at his flesh. When all of his bullets were spent the terrified outlaw tried to use the weapon as a club. It made no difference; the jaws of the creature gripped down on his throat and shook him as though he were nothing more than a rag doll.

The horrifying scream filled the clearing as claws and fangs ended the life of the mayor of San Angelo. Then the screaming ended and the wolf was gone into the misty timberland above the corral.

Only Iron Eyes had seen the wolf clearly from beside the log cabin, from where, through the cracks in its bolted door, he could hear the whimpering of a child. The bounty hunter shook spent casings from one of his Navy Colts and was about to reload the hot weapon when the door to one of the larger buildings swung open. Bathed in coal-tar light, a burly man appeared. He was carrying a scattergun.

The large man saw the pitiful figure of Iron Eyes and swung the double-barrelled weapon until he had the bounty hunter in his sights. Faster than most men could even spit, Iron Eyes reached down, dragged his Bowie knife from the neck of his left boot and threw it. Then he turned away.

Both barrels of the scattergun exploded their fiery venom as the large blade of the knife went straight into the outlaw's chest.

Peppered by buckshot, the bounty hunter slowly staggered to the body and pulled his knife out of the dead man. He wiped its blade along his pants leg, then looked to the corral again as he slid the long blade down into its hiding-place. He was about to advance when he saw Squirrel Sally riding down the road astride his palomino stallion. Smoke billowed from the barrel of her Winchester. She reined in beside the body of what had once been the mayor of San Angelo. What was left was only recognizable by his fancy clothes.

'Is ya OK, Iron Eyes?' she called out.

'I bin better.' The bounty hunter returned to the cabin and looked at the padlock. He finished reloading his gun, then shot the lock clean off the sturdy door. The gun was dropped into his deep pocket.

Cautiously Iron Eyes pulled the door open and

heard the frightened child sobbing in a darkened corner of the cabin. He remained in the shadows, hiding his face from the already alarmed girl, and beckoned with a long thin arm. Even though he realized that the little daughter of his friend probably did not speak English he still spoke to her.

'Don't cry none, little 'un. I ain't gonna harm ya none. Come here. Ya father is close. Come with me, gal,' Iron Eyes urged in a tone which somehow soothed the alarmed girl. She moved to the long thin man and took his skeletal hand.

They walked slowly away from the log cabin, which had been her prison for so long, towards the tall palomino and the tiny female perched on its saddle. Sally said nothing as she watched the incongruous pair walking towards her.

Then out of the trees Silent Wolf swiftly emerged and raced to his daughter. The chief lifted the girl up in his arms and held her, sobbing, in his powerful arms. His eyes looked at the bounty hunter.

'You are my brother, Iron Eyes. The bravest of the brave.'

A wry smile etched his scarred features. 'I seen me a wolf come down here and kill that varmint, *amigo*. Ya wouldn't happen to know anything about that, would ya?'

'There are many wolves in this forest,' Silent Wolf said, and gave a whistle. Both Sally and Iron Eyes watched as the chief's pinto pony appeared from the trees and trotted down to where its master stood holding his daughter.

'Well, one of them sure took a dislike to this fancy dude, old friend,' Iron Eyes observed as he turned to face the warrior. 'Or was it a man who can change into a wolf?'

Silent Wolf said nothing. He placed his daughter on the back of the pinto, then threw himself up behind her. He nodded at the weary bounty hunter and tapped his heels. The pony galloped away and soon vanished in the mist that was hanging a few feet above the road.

Sally leaned over from her lofty perch and grabbed the hair of the bounty hunter. She tugged it hard enough for Iron Eyes to yelp.

'Leave me be, Squirrel. I'm kinda worn out.'

She frowned. 'I reckon ya must have a fever. Ya still gabbing on about him being a wolf, Iron Eyes. Ain't healthy to talk like a madman, ya know? Folks will think ya loco.'

Iron Eyes pushed her back on to the high saddle cantle and mounted his horse. He gathered up the reins and looked over his shoulder into her face.

'I ain't loco. I seen me a wolf.'

'But a man can't change into no wolf, ya locobean.' Sally scowled.

Iron Eyes vainly searched his pockets for a cigar.

'Locobean am I? OK. If'n ya so damn smart, can ya figure out how come my old pal's face and hands was covered in blood if he didn't change into a wolf, Squirrel gal? That blood weren't his own. He didn't have a scratch on him so how come he had blood on him? Answer me that if ya can.'

Then the young female saw something and tapped his shoulders. Her tiny trigger finger pointed as she slid the Winchester back under the saddle.

'Do ya see what I sees?' she asked.

Iron Eyes looked to where she was pointing. Three wolves came out of the brush close to the road and ran up the road. The road along which the pinto had only just travelled.

'Damn it all. Wolves,' Iron Eyes gasped.

'Real wolves,' Sally whispered and slapped the back of his head. 'Not the kind locobeans talks about. Real four-legged ones. There's ya damn answer. Ya seen a real wolf.'

Iron Eyes gathered up his reins. 'Then how come he had blood on himself?'

She slapped his head again. 'Shut up. I'm tuckered.'

She wrapped her arms around his waist, rested her head on his back and sighed. Iron Eyes tapped his spurs.

'Where we going, honeychild?' she asked her exhausted companion.

'To find us some cigars and a barrel of whiskey.'

'Ya just a romantic old dog,' she purred.

Iron Eyes steered the stallion towards the road. Then felt both her hands slide into his pants pockets. Her fingers wriggled and the bounty hunter shook his head. He was too tired to fight any longer.

He spurred.